CA
IS
JO}_

MW01256940

"Very few detective stories baffle me nowadays, but Mr. Carr's always do."

— Agatha Christie

"One of the three or four best detective story writers since Poe."

— Edmund Crispin

JOHN DICKSON CARR
Available in Library of Crime Classics® editions

Dr. Gideon Fell Novels:
BELOW SUSPICION
HAG'S NOOK
HE WHO WHISPERS
THE HOUSE AT SATAN'S ELBOW
THE PROBLEM OF THE GREEN CAPSULE
THE SLEEPING SPHINX
THE THREE COFFINS
TIL DEATH DO US PART

Non-series:
THE BURNING COURT

Writing as Carter Dickson
Sir Henry Merrivale Novels:
THE GILDED MAN
HE WOULDN'T KILL PATIENCE
THE JUDAS WINDOW
NINE – AND DEATH MAKES TEN
THE PEACOCK FEATHER MURDERS
THE PUNCH AND JUDY MURDERS
THE RED WIDOW MURDERS

Douglas G. Greene, series consultant

THE
GILDED MAN

A CRIME CLASSIC

INTERNATIONAL POLYGONICS, LTD.
NEW YORK CITY

THE GILDED MAN

Library of Congress Card Catalog No. 88-82353
ISBN 0-930330-88-9

Printed and manufactured in the United States
of America.
First IPL printing November 1988.
10 9 8 7 6 5 4 3 2 1

1

And this," said Betty, "is The Little Theater."

Reaching inside the door, she switched on one panel of lights after another. Her companion looked in, and felt—not for the first time—that he had got into a chapter of the *Arabian Nights*.

"They had gaslight then, of course," Betty added. "Otherwise it's much the same."

"This is where she gave her private theatricals?"

"Yes. And this is where she died."

Lined and cushioned like a jewel-box, the miniature theater glowed. Its heavy velvet curtains shut out sound and light. Its colors were somber gray and gold. Some forty feet across, it was circular in shape, with curious carven frettings. The stage alone made a straight line against the round walls, at what might be called the front of it. This stage seemed little more than a carpeted dais inside a gilt-fretted arch. The seats were a few armchairs at the back, behind wooden box-railings woven in front with the monogram, "F.V." It breathed of the eighteen-sixties—

"Except for *that*," Betty supplied, and pointed.

Nicholas Wood laughed. Immediately afterwards he wondered whether he should not have uttered a sympathetic grunt instead, for the girl seemed annoyed.

Into one wall of the theater had been set a tiny but complete modern bar. Its bottles and glasses gleamed against mirrors; it was even equipped with such facetious signs as, "No checks accepted," and, "Betting strictly prohibited."

"That's father's idea," Betty explained. She made a face. "He never had an idea that wasn't practical. He's even put a motion-picture projector behind that wall over there. You can run down a screen inside the stage, if you want to."

"And your mother?"

"Oh, mother was furious. Still—!"

Nicholas Wood found it hard to realize that he was on the top floor of a country house not twenty miles from London, with snow sifting over the roofs and the gurgle of central heating never far away. Bar or no, this miniature theater had an air about it. Its padded quiet, its furtive splendor and dream-like aloofness, made you walk softly and speak in a whisper.

Betty Stanhope saw that its atmosphere impressed him. And this, he felt, pleased her.

The problem he found here did not concern her, at least. Betty was frankly a romantic: frankly one who loved the picturesque, the elaborate. Not that she showed this, either in dress or behavior.

She was a soft-voiced, serious-faced girl in her middle twenties, with a lurking smile which surprised you. That smile lit up her face and eyes. You had realized before that she was pretty, in the conventional sense of good features and rather wax-bloom complexion. She wore her brown hair in a page-boy bob; her blue eyes were straightforward. But the occasional smile, curving round her lips, brought out a quality which some might have called a sense of humor and others a sense of devilment. It flashed out; then the face grew blank again.

Wearing a plain black dinner dress, without jewelry, she stood in the middle of the secret theater, and nodded to herself as though she liked to see everything in place.

"Anyway, since the bar *is* here"—Betty smiled—"would you care for a drink?"

"Thanks."

Betty opened the flap of the bar-counter, and slid into the niche. A conical lamp over the bar, the brightest light in this dim room, shone down on brown hair touched with gold. Nick studied the gilded monogram, "F.V.," worked into the wall below the counter.

" 'Flavia Venner,' " he said. "You say she died here?"

"Yes. She dropped dead during a performance of *Salomé*."

"*Salomé?*"

"That's right. It was a special play written for her by—" Betty named a Victorian poet so eminent that mention of his name was like mention of the Abbey in which he lay buried. She saw her companion's startled look.

"Yes, it's quite true. We have the manuscript down in the library. Whisky or brandy?"

"Whisky, thanks. Was it . . . ?"

"It was just what you think it was. There was a dreadful scandal, of course. But they hushed it up. In those days they had the decent belief that it didn't matter what you did, provided only you did it discreetly."

The bar contained a row of bottles upended in racks, with little taps like a real public-house. Betty turned off the tap of the whisky. She seemed rather defiant about the way in which she pushed glass and soda-syphon across to him.

"And you agree with that?"

Betty considered this.

"Yes, I think I do. But my sister wouldn't agree, I'm afraid."

(No, he thought, Eleanor wouldn't agree.)

"Eleanor would say," the girl went on, "that it didn't matter what you did, provided only you did it indiscreetly. To show you had no complexes." She made a little face, and then laughed. "Yes, you're right. I hate that word."

"Complex?"

"Yes. It seems to express everything that's new and shiny and knowing and tiresome."

And so he spoke lightly, though he realized he was more than half serious in asking the question.

"You mean you're a Victorian yourself? In spirit?"

"Hardly that. But I agree with my father in disliking fads, at least. As anybody will tell you, he never had an idea that wasn't practical."

"I wonder," said Nicholas Wood.

He had made a blunder.

He saw this reflected in her face, in the quick turn of the blue eyes. The words had slipped out; he had been staring at his drink, absently; he had been off-guard. For her part, Betty had been polishing a glass, with a competently professional air, but her fingers stopped. They looked at each other. Then he tilted his own glass, and drank.

"Why did you say that?" Betty asked directly.

"Say what?"

"About my father?"

"My dear Miss Stanhope! I was only wondering about the habits of money-kings."

"Oh?"

"Here's your father, with millions to his credit . . ."

"Not that much."

"Well! A few thousands, anyhow." He put down the glass. "And here, as a monument to it, is this house: where you press a button, and anything can happen. I was only wondering whether people like that ever make mistakes."

His heels sank into the thick gray carpet. The dim lights in the theater lurked behind wall-prisms, edging the gilt reliefs with shadows. Betty's face, though strongly illuminated from above, grew difficult to read. That sense of communication with her, which he had felt all evening, was gone like her eager

7

friendliness. Leaving off cleaning the glass, she fell to polishing the bar with the same cloth.

"Flavia Venner," she observed, "used to call this place Masque House."

"Why?"

"Never mind." Betty looked up. "Mr. Wood, who are you?"

"That," he said, "is a difficult question for anybody to answer. All of a sudden, I mean."

"Please don't joke with me!"

"I'm not joking. I'm—" he wanted to turn away from her super-feminine directness—"I'm a friend of your father's. He invited me here for New Year's. You're a good deal like him, Miss Stanhope."

She eyed the counter. "Do you know my father well?"

"Yes; quite well."

"Yet you didn't know," said Betty, "that he isn't really my father at all? That both he and my mother were married before? That Eleanor is his daughter by his first marriage, and I'm my mother's child by *her* first marriage? You're a close friend of his; but you didn't know that?"

There *was* a sound in the room—the ticking of a small clock behind the bar, whose hands pointed to twenty minutes past ten.

Nick laughed.

"I referred," he said, "to your methods. Direct, aren't they?"

She looked so miserable that he instantly regretted having said it. How, he wondered, had the conversation got into this queer channel? How could you tell the point at which you strayed from intimacy and got into a jungle?

"And if you doubt my bona fides," he added, "Vincent James can vouch for me."

(A good thing, he reflected, having Vincent James in the house. If Vince said, in that lordly way of his, 'Nick Wood? I know him. He's all right,' then the most uneasy host or hostess would be reassured.)

Betty spoke abruptly.

"Please forgive me. I seem to be talking the most awful rot, and being rude into the bargain."

"Not at all. Tell me about Flavia Venner."

"Are you interested? Really interested?"

"Very much so."

Betty leaned her elbows on the polished counter. The lamp overhead kindled golden touches in her light brown hair. Her eyes wandered round the theater, while her mouth moved as though she hesitated about how to begin.

8

"This was her house," Betty answered. "Lord Saxmunden bought it for her in the middle sixties."

"She was a famous actress?"

Betty lifted one eyebrow. "Say notorious rather than famous. Though she thought herself a cut above the 'vulgar' actress and wanted to play a classic repertoire. But they didn't go to see that: they went to see Venner. The private theatricals here, according to tradition, were patronized by royalty."

Here he had a sudden mad vision of the late lamented Queen Victoria hobbling into this theater, looking round grimly, and announcing that she was not amused.

Again the flicker of mirth crossed Betty's face as she evidently guessed his thought.

"No, no! I mean lesser royalty. Even so, the conventions were preserved. Do you know what a beignoir is?"

He searched his mind.

"They have them in French theaters, haven't they?" he asked. "It's a private box, a sort of cell with a hole cut in the wall, where people in mourning can go to the performance without being observed."

Betty nodded.

"Come and see ours," she invited.

Raising the flap of the counter, she slipped outside and walked across the theater. He followed her. She passed the rail-shielded armchairs on their raised platform, and went to the rear wall. To his eyes the heavy velvet curtains looked no different from the curtains in any other part of the wall. But Betty pulled one of them aside, revealing a dark niche. As the curtain was drawn wider, he saw a heavy cushioned seat, almost as broad as a couch, set on another raised platform in a padded alcove.

"Your august personage," she explained, "could sit here in seclusion and discretion."

"But how did the august personage manage to see out?"

"Try it," Betty invited.

Intrigued, he stepped into the alcove and sat down. Betty came after him. Her arm moved, and the curtain snakily closed. Darkness descended like an extinguisher-cap, except for a narrow oblong opening—at about the level of their eyes—through which he could see the stage opposite as though through gray-woven gauze.

"It's a trick in the weave of the curtain," she went on. "You don't notice it at all unless a strong light's thrown on the place."

A room within a room, an alcove within an alcove. From where he sat he had a good view through the stage to the marble

9

mantelpiece at its rear. By craning his neck to the right he could even see the bar, intruding modernity with colored labels.

"There were several of them," Betty said. "Father took the middle one, the biggest, for the motion-picture projector. Stuffy in here, isn't it?"

This was the point at which the back of his hand happened to touch Betty's side.

So light a touch, so casual and accidental a touch, can arouse emotions out of all proportion to the fact of what is done. It can suggest. It can bring thoughts where no such thoughts existed before.

Through Nicholas Wood's mind flashed the remembrance that he was here not as a guest: that his plans entailed a sort of treachery against Dwight Stanhope and Dwight Stanhope's worldly goods.

But he could not help himself. He could hear—almost feel—Betty's light breathing beside him. Darkness, the room within a room, the close musty brocade of the alcove, brought a train of suggestions only completed by the touch against the girl's side. A faint glow filtered through the opening in the curtain. As Betty turned her head, quickly, he could just see one of her eyes; and it looked frightened. He knew that the same realization had come to her, with the same unexpectedness.

"We'd better . . ." she began abruptly, and stopped.

Waiting.

That was it: They were both waiting. What are you going to do? Well, what are *you* going to do? Are you thinking what I'm thinking? Or is this an idea I hold alone? Under such circumstances, in such wordless conversations, seconds—half a second—can seem like minutes.

He dropped his hand, and it fell on her hand. She did not draw it away; but then she did not move at all. The broadcloth shoulder of his dinner jacket was against the thin black tulle which covered her arm.

He felt the movement of her breathing. And, as he turned towards her, a new and unexpected voice startled them by speaking out clearly in the theater.

"*Hullo!*" said the new voice. "*Somebody's left the lights on in here.*"

10

2

It is to be recorded that Betty started as though she had been burnt. But Nick, putting out his hand to steady himself, and to avoid falling outwards through the curtains like a body in a detective story, peered round sharply to the right.

"Steady," he muttered in her ear. "It's only Vince—no, by George, it's your father."

"All right," pursued the mild voice of Dwight Stanhope. "What have you got to say to me?"

Dwight Stanhope, in his middle fifties, had the vigor and alertness of a man twenty years younger. They saw his well-tailored back as he came into their line of vision; he strolled across to the bar, turned round, and put his elbow on the counter.

He usually stood upright, tall and without any spare flesh. His hair was of that color commonly called iron-gray, but which more nearly resembles unwashed lamb's wool. His eye, voice, and manner were all mild, even gentle, though his high color suggested blood-pressure.

"Hullo!" he added, picking up the empty glass from the counter, and sniffing at it. "Somebody's been drinking here."

"Everybody's drinking," retorted his companion, a little thin man with a semi-bald head. "Don't like it. Bad for 'em."

"Oh, they'll be all right."

"Your daughter's drinking too much. And you know it."

"Which daughter?" smiled Dwight Stanhope.

"Eleanor, of course. You didn't think I meant Betty? Betty's a nice girl."

At this point, if not before, Betty Stanhope and Nicholas Wood should have come out of the alcove.

On paper, it looks easy. You just step out and say, "Excuse us; we were studying the effect of the theater with the curtains closed." But when your guilty conscience tells you that this wasn't what you meditated at all, and that guilt will be manifest in your face, it produces a certain indecision.

Especially so, Nick thought, in front of Mr. Buller Naseby.

The small, thin, quick-moving man he identified as Mr. Naseby. Mr. Naseby, who had appeared at dinner that night and talked of little except his digestion, was not staying here. His own country house, it appeared, was only a quarter of a mile away; and he was another financier whose credit in the City stood almost as high as Dwight Stanhope's.

Betty, so powerfully embarrassed that she had turned her head away, did in fact make a half-hearted effort to leave the alcove. Her companion restrained her. For—if the truth must be told—he had another reason.

Through the gauze opening, they watched.

"What's all this," said Mr. Naseby, hauling himself up on a bar-stool and entwining his legs with it, "about a New Year's party?"

"That's what we call it."

"New Year's party!" said Mr. Naseby. "Damn silly idea, if you ask me."

Dwight Stanhope smiled slightly.

"Not a bit of it. My wife wanted to give a Christmas party, with masquerade. If there's anything in the world I dislike, it's getting dressed up."

Mr. Naseby's grunt conceded this point, though he did not seem so sure of it as his host.

"Furthermore," pursued Stanhope, "Christmas parties mean mess; and I'm not fond of mess. As it is, I get off lightly."

"You're a canny swine, young Dwight," observed Mr. Naseby without rancor.

"Thanks. Besides, it isn't, properly speaking, a party at all. We've got only two guests—Vincent James and young Wood. I wanted the Commander to come over, but he's still on maneuvers."

"Vincent James," said Mr. Naseby. "The eternal diner-out. If that chap couldn't week-end with somebody, he'd blow his brains out from sheer boredom. Do you realize, young Dwight, that you and I work our guts loose to provide meals for what they call the nobility and gentry? Just like French chefs?"

Stanhope considered this. He seemed about to add something, but he checked himself.

"*And* our families," Stanhope pointed out. "What else can we do?"

"Chefs!" said Mr. Naseby bitterly. "That's what we are. Chefs!"

Stanhope grinned at him.

"Come off it, young Buller," he said. "You don't work your guts loose. You don't even work hard. You only work at all because, otherwise, you wouldn't know what to do with yourself. You're a fraud."

"And you hate frauds?"

"As ever," nodded Stanhope.

"Bah," said Mr. Naseby. There was a saucer of potato chips

12

on the counter, and he picked up one. "This fellow Wood. What do you know about *him?*"

"Not much. He's a friend of Betty's. She picked him up in London somewhere, and seemed keen to have me invite him down here. That's all."

There was a silence.

Betty turned her head slowly round to stare at her companion.

As he told this flat lie, Dwight Stanhope again leaned one elbow negligently on the counter. Even this seemed a derogation of dignity for him. His mild, candid eyes were incurious. Then he brushed the subject aside as lightly as he might have brushed a grain of salt from the counter. When he spoke again, a new note seemed to have crept into the conversation.

"What did you want to talk to me about?" he asked.

"Eh? Talk to you about?"

"Up here. In private."

Mr. Naseby champed a potato chip, and was silent for some time. They could see the back of his skull, with what remained of his rather long, gray-black hair plastered against it.

"Have you thought about my proposition?"

"Which particular proposition?"

"The gilded man," answered Mr. Naseby.

The smile on Dwight Stanhope's face was one of skepticism but ineffable kindliness. He seemed to commiserate with an old friend. He shook his head.

"Buller, old man! You didn't mean that seriously?"

"And why not?"

"You—a practical business man?"

"I *am* a practical business man," said Mr. Naseby, whacking the edge of the counter. "That's why I say it can be done."

"'The gilded man,'" quoted Stanhope. His words became still more cryptic. "One proper exploration of the pool, and all our troubles are over. Have you gone back to reading schoolboy romances? No, no, no. And it would cost . . . I forget what it would cost?"

Mr. Naseby was dogged.

"You don't forget. You've seen the figures. But I'll tell you again. Fifty, sixty thousand."

Dwight Stanhope made a grimace of distress.

"Fifty, sixty thousand," insisted Mr. Naseby, "to do the job properly."

"Well! If you think it's such a good gamble, why don't you back it yourself?"

13

"Share-the-risk," said Mr. Naseby, shaking his head violently. "Always the best principle. You ought to know that. It's been your game. Share the risk; and then get out with the profits while the getting's good."

"Sorry, old man. But I can't share the risk in any such venture as that. There's only one gilded man *I'm* after."

"Young Dwight," said Mr. Naseby abruptly, "can I ask a question?"

"Of course."

"Are you hard up?"

Stanhope still leaned negligently, his right hand clasping the fingers of his left. While they were discussing business, his smile had remained fixed and printed and rather false. But this last question seemed genuinely to amuse him.

"No," he said. "Not more than the rest of us, anyway. Why do you ask?"

"You're acting damned funny, then," said the blunt Mr. Naseby.

"As—how?"

"Pictures."

"I don't understand."

"You've got a collection of pictures." Perched like a monkey on the bar-stool, Mr. Naseby took up another potato chip. They could not see his face; but the back of his skull was eloquent. "Very valuable. Or so they tell me. Don't understand such things myself. Most of 'em beionged to that old trollop . . . what was her name?"

"Flavia Venner?"

"That's it. Flavia Venner. They're insured, I suppose. Bound to be. If they're not, you're a fool."

Stanhope made no comment.

"Those pictures *used* to be well protected," continued his guest. "Upstairs gallery. Burglar alarms galore."

"Well?"

"But what do you do now? You take the most valuable of 'em downstairs. You hang 'em in the dining room. No burglar alarms at all. French windows opening on the lawn. Young Dwight, why don't you stick your head out and whistle for Bill Sikes? Or do you by any chance *want* the pictures to be stolen? I only ask as an old friend. Don't understand such things myself."

After this string of sentences, Mr. Naseby began to eat chips with such rapidity that he emptied the saucer. The crunching noise seemed to underline what he said. Dwight Stanhope watched him with a pleasant, expressionless face.

14

"No," he agreed. "You don't."

"That's the first item," said Mr. Naseby, wiping salt off his mouth. "The second item . . ."

"Boo!" said a voice, with shattering effect, immediately behind his ear.

Eleanor Stanhope, appearing out of the gloom, threw her arms round Mr. Naseby's shoulders and gave Mr. Naseby a smacking kiss on the bald part of his head. When he twisted his head round to peer at her, rather like a turtle, she added another moist kiss above one shaggy eyebrow.

"Where on earth have you two people got to?" she demanded. "Christabel wants you to play Monopoly or something. And where's Betty and that good-looking young explorer?"

"Mr. Wood is not an explorer, my dear," said Dwight mildly.

"I feel people," declared Eleanor, "in spiritual auras. Or is it auræ? I never was any bloody good at plurals. If he's not an explorer, he ought to be."

"Better sit down," Mr. Naseby said unkindly, "before you fall down."

"That," said Eleanor, "is not nice. I think I should like another drink, please."

Nobody stirred.

Eleanor sighed. "In that case, I suppose I've got to get it myself." She became polite. "You don't mind if I have another drink, father?"

"No. Of course not."

(But he did mind.)

Eleanor, at least one watcher had to admit, held her liquor well. She was not loud: at most, you could say she was audible. She spoke quietly, with a brightness about the eyes and a certain offhandedness; you liked her even when you wanted to wallop her.

Moving round behind the bar, she surveyed them gravely. In person she was one of those girls who seem lacquered or polished from head to foot. She had a dark complexion, with a tawny sort of skin, black hair, and brown eyes against strongly luminous whites. Comparing the two, you could see her resemblance to Dwight Stanhope. She was smaller than Betty; perhaps two or three years older than her step-sister; and she wore white, with pearls, as though in contrast to Betty's black.

"What'll it be, gentlemen?" inquired Eleanor, breathing like a distillery.

"Nothing for me, thanks," said her father.

"Nor me," said Mr. Naseby.

Eleanor's forehead turned mutinous. But she did not snap out at them, as might have been expected. Instead she quietly turned the tap twice, for a double whisky, and set it neat on the counter.

"Father"—she smiled—"won't give up his allegiance to eating fruit and keeping fit. And dear old Mr. Naseby . . . potato chips."

"Be quiet," said Naseby.

"For shame," said Eleanor. "Your digestion. Dirty saucer!"

Snatching up the empty saucer, she switched on a water-tap under the bar and held it there. The water, circling in thin spray, splashed back against her white dress. As though this had given her an idea, she grew intent; she turned the water partly off, and let the saucer fill to the brim. Then she placed the full saucer on the counter.

"Do you know what that means?" she demanded.

Naseby was impatient and Dwight was puzzled.

"Means?"

"Yes. If I were dead—or dying—"

"Eleanor," said Dwight very quietly.

It was a piece of byplay which they did not understand: at least, until long afterwards. Eleanor started to laugh, but thought better of it. She had herself in hand like powder packed into a cartridge. About her there was a hard brightness, of muscles stung with alcohol.

"I'm sorry!" she added, with such evidently honest contrition that her two companions relaxed. "Bit off my feed tonight, I expect. Well, here's luck. Here's to the New Year, nineteen-thirty-nine. And what it brings."

She drained the glass.

"It'll bring no good." Nasbey's tone was sour. "I warn you, it'll bring no good."

"Oh, I don't know," said Dwight. "If we can keep out these infernal Communists . . . ."

"And now for item two," said Eleanor. As the flush of the whisky rose, it was as though a wheel went round behind her eyes. "Item one," she checked on her fingers,' "why does my father keep his paintings in a place where they're not safe? Just as I heard you saying a minute ago."

Dwight and Naseby glanced sharply at each other.

"Item two," pursued Eleanor. "Why is an effort being made to arrange a marriage between me, *moi qui vous parle*, and the very rich Commander Dawson?"

She reflected.

16

"Mind you, not that I'd object to marrying Pinkey Dawson. It might be rather fun."

"Marriage, young woman," snarled Mr. Naseby, "is not fun."

"You're telling me?" said Eleanor.

"I mean—!"

"You see, it's blighted love, really. I'd marry Vince James like a shot, if he'd have me. Only he won't. So why not Pinkey? Why not dear Buller, even? Wouldn't you have me, Buller?"

She twinkled her eyes at Mr. Naseby, who appeared shocked.

"But if anybody tells you that Victorian marriages can't be 'arranged' today, you take my tip and don't believe 'em. It does seem unfair, in a way. Why pick on me? Why not choose Betty? She'd love it. She's a natural wife. I've sometimes wondered whether she's ever . . . ."

The perverseness of events took control here. The perverseness of events decreed that Nicholas Wood, in shifting his position, should kick against the curtain so that it moved.

"Hell!" he said to himself, not loudly.

The position of these two behind the curtain had already become ridiculous, and was fast growing intolerable. It was hot in there. Dust settled. They both wanted to cough.

In the hush Eleanor's voice rose.

"Ever done anything she shouldn't," Eleanor concluded very thoughtfully. Her over-bright eyes were on the curtain.

"Shall we go downstairs?" suggested Dwight.

"Yes, let's!" Eleanor hurried out from behind the bar, stumbled against it, and righted herself. "I was just wondering," she added, "whether I left my cigarette case . . ."

And she was coming straight towards the hiding-place.

In the background, these two could see Dwight's easy posture, his right hand still clasping the fingers of his left. Mr. Naseby turned round a wrinkled face to look over one shoulder. And Nick reflected that, if he knew anything at all of women, Betty wouldn't blame Eleanor for the drench of embarrassment about to burst over them: she would blame him.

A measure of tipsy craft marked Eleanor's actions. She first looked closely at the armchairs of the miniature theater. They could see her laughing face, the pearls swaying against the tawny skin, the frantically impish eyes.

"Cigarette case," she kept muttering. "Cigarette case. Cigarette case."

Rounding the dais, she swept close to the curtains. Her head turned, and she gave a casual glance through. She could not have seen much against the light, but she saw enough. Her eyes

17

opened wide in an expression so profoundly delighted that it was like the expression of a child.

Then Eleanor Stanhope did something for which one man could have wrung her hands in gratitude. She turned away.

"No," she said aloud. "It's not here. There's nothing here. Shall we go downstairs?"

Taking her father by one arm and Mr. Buller Naseby by the other, she marched between them to the door. Her head reached only to the level of her father's shoulder, but it was on a level with that of Mr. Naseby—who seemed uncomfortably and unaccountably shy. She did not look again towards the curtains. But, as they went out, her delighted voice rose up with impish clearness.

"I *still* say that fellow's an explorer."

3

In the drawing room downstairs, Christabel Stanhope sat and talked to Vincent James. Or, to be more exact, Christabel talked while James threw dice and listened.

"Let me see," mused Christabel. "What's today?"

"Thursday."

"Then Saturday will be New Year's Eve. And New Year's Eve is our real entertainment. The children hereabouts look forward to it so much."

"Sort of yearly feature?"

"Yes. In the theater upstairs. We've got a conjuror this year, and I think a lightning-cartoonist too. It's no good Dwight trying to be the country squire, because Mr. Radlett's got all that taped. But at least we can give them entertainment." Christabel paused. "I suppose you've wondered, Mr. James, why my husband ever bought a house like this?"

"Good Lord, no!"

"It's ridiculous and over-dressed," said Christabel, fishing. "I know people say so, behind my back."

"You're imagining things."

Christabel glanced round the long, lofty room. In Flavia Venner's day, this room had been copied from a Venetian villa. Even then the architect must have sensed that white and pink-mottled marble is apt to seem chilly against an English climate. Tapestry panels had been let into the walls; the marble mausoleum of a fireplace contained a log-fire big enough to have burnt a Renaissance heretic; subdued lighting outlined the

18

comfort of modern furniture and threw the Doges' magnificence into shadow.

Beyond, past a broad arch, was the dining room. This was dark except for the little hood of yellow light over each of the paintings which hung there.

There were only four of these paintings, four cores of illuminated color against the walls, yet they caught the eye with disturbing hypnosis. Flavia Venner had been fascinated by the Spanish painters, by what can only be called the burning quality of their work. From where she sat now by the fireplace in the drawing room, Christabel could just see the small El Greco, unique among that artist's subjects, which hung above the sideboard.

Christabel took a cigarette out of a box at her elbow. Vincent James instantly had a match in front of it.

"Thanks. I imagine you know," she went on, inhaling deeply, "that I was on the stage once?"

"I should think so! I used to see you when I was a boy at sch—" He coughed suddenly, and stopped. "That is, a few years ago."

"You're not offending me," said Christabel. "It *was* a long time ago."

"I was your great fan then. I still am."

Christabel eyed him shrewdly.

"Flattery. Gross flattery. But I like it."

The heat of the fire, a dazzling wall, fanned their eyelids. James returned to his dice at the backgammon table.

Christabel was thinking: So this is the man Eleanor's fallen for. This is the fellow who's so much in demand at week-ends for social desirability plus cricket, plus shooting, plus a passionless and almost inhuman skill at all kinds of sport.

Well, he wasn't inhuman. A bit stupid, perhaps. A bit arrogant sometimes. But of retiring manner, with an engaging presence and a habit of taking himself so much for granted that he pleased everybody. Thirty-two or so. As tall as Dwight; square jaw, cleft chin, tight-curling light hair, inquiring smile.

The smile was even more inquiring now.

"Penny, Mrs. Stanhope?"

This, in short, is the man for whom Eleanor has fallen; and he—honest English gentleman—is in the depths of being conscience-stricken because he can't see her for beans.

Christabel laughed aloud.

"Is it as funny as all that, Mrs. Stanhope?"

"Sorry." Christabel felt a little ashamed of herself. "I was thinking . . ."

19

"What?"

"Oh, about Dwight living in Flavia Venner's house. Dwight couldn't even be persuaded to give a masquerade. He hates fancy dress. But he bought me the house because he knew I wanted it."

It was true. Dwight Stanhope had married her when he was twenty-five, a widower without two shillings to his name; and he had worshipped her ever since. Christabel watched curling cigarette smoke. A word of advice, suitably served up, might not be out of place here.

She gestured with the cigarette.

"You see, Flavia Venner was always my great heroine. To own her house had been the dream of my life. Flavia Venner carried everything in the grand manner. She did as she pleased and, if you'll excuse me, just didn't gave a damn. Like . . ."

Vincent James stiffened.

Christabel guessed that he disliked intimate conversations: disliked anything that savored of the confidential. But he could not resist this.

"Like Eleanor, were you going to say?"

"No," replied Christabel. "Not like Eleanor." There was a pause. "Take my advice, Mr. James. Never have two grown daughters, one of them a step-daughter."

"Thanks," said the other, rattling the dice vigorously in the box. "I'll remember that."

"You see, you have to be fair to both of them. Betty is my own daughter. Naturally, I'm prejudiced in her favor."

"Naturally."

"But they've both been treated alike. We've brought them up in what's called the modern manner. They've done as they liked. Dwight has never interfered in anything, never said one word, even when you could feel disapproval oozing from him clear across the room. And, believe me, Dwight's 'I-am-not-fond-of' something is as strong as anybody else's uppercut to the jaw."

(Am I talking like a schoolmarm? Eleanor would say so. Yet it's true, every word of it.)

"Eleanor," Christabel went on, "Eleanor's a clever girl. But she's got a hair-trigger mind and hair-trigger emotions. Often she thinks she wants something when she's only bored. Do you understand me?"

"N-no, I can't say I do."

(My God, you're even stupider than I thought!)

But there was no time to continue. Eleanor herself, holding tightly to the arm of Mr. Buller Naseby, arrived flushed in the room and hurried her captive into the firelight.

20

Christabel sat back in the big chair by the carven fireplace. From behind the lamp on the table beside her, she fished out her glass of brandy and drank again, wondering if her loquacity had been due to the brandy. At fifty-four, Christabel still had the figure of a girl. Patches of clear silver hair can blend well with brown, as though they had been painted there in a sort of super beauty-treatment.

"I've collared these two," Eleanor announced, nodding over her shoulder towards Dwight in the background. "They'll play Monopoly or Postman's Knock or anything you like."

Christabel swallowed brandy.

"It's rather late to play anything," she said. "Half past eleven."

"It is," said Mr. Naseby. "I'll ring for my car, if you don't mind. Got to get up early in the morning."

"Eleanor, where's Betty? And Mr. Wood?"

Eleanor's glee convulsed her.

"I really don't know." She spoke with radiant innocence. "They're probably exploring the house on the track of Flavia Venner. Or out cavorting in the snow like a pair of innocents."

"It's not snowing," growled Mr. Naseby, a stickler for accuracy. "Only a few flakes. Too cold to snow."

Eleanor brushed this aside. She said:

"Anyway, I think I should like a game of some kind. I was telling father and Oliver Cromwell here—" the thought flashed through Christabel's mind that Buller Naseby did look rather like a Puritan father—"about my ambition. I'd like to invent a new game. I'd like to invent a new thrill."

"Why?" asked Christabel.

Eleanor's voice grew shrill.

"Because I'm fed up, with the world and everything in it. I've seen everything. I've done everything. . . ."

"Do you really think that?" inquired Christabel, with interest but without surprise. "I used to think so myself, once."

"Or nearly everything," Eleanor corrected herself. "Of course, I might commit a murder."

Christabel finished her brandy.

"The trouble with that is," she said, "that they always catch you and hang you. It's not worth the trouble and risk, even when you've got a motive."

'And besides," put in Dwight, standing rigid but falling in with his wife's mood, "you're forgetting one main point about murder."

"Which is?"

"That the wrong person always gets murdered," answered Dwight.

Eleanor gritted her teeth. "You won't rise to the bait, will you? Well, you never can tell. Maybe there are all kinds of dreadful things in this house, with Flavia Venner's ghost to inspire 'em. Maybe that young explorer is murdering Betty at this minute. Maybe Betty herself, or anybody else, has a guilty secret that mustn't come out. I'm going to find *something* interesting in this world, so help me! Speaking of something interesting, what about a nightcap?"

"If you like," shrugged Christabel.

"Jolly good idea," agreed Vincent James.

Buller Naseby was distinctly heard to observe that some people's children ought to be smacked. Without so much as looking at James, Eleanor moved round the sofa on which he was sitting, and inspected a side table there.

"Christabel, you fiend!" She held up and waggled a cut-glass decanter. "You've finished it!"

"You yourself, my dear—" Dwight began.

"I'll ring. No, the servants are in bed. Never mind. Dining room. Sideboard. Come along, Cromwell."

Impetuously dragging Naseby with her, she hurried across towards the dining room.

Dwight Stanhope watched them go. James threw dice, with a small rattle. Christabel finished her cigarette and threw it into the fire.

"Christabel," said Dwight, smiling at her with a long, slow scrutiny, "shall I tell you something?" He put out his hand, and his wife took it. "Shall I tell you why you're such a remarkable person?"

"La, sir!"

"I mean it. Don't mind us, Mr. James."

"Not at all, not at all!"

"I *will* have brandy!" squeaked out Eleanor's voice from the dining room, with rising fury. "I don't care whether it's mixing 'em or not! I *will* have brandy!"

"Excuse me," said Dwight—and followed Eleanor.

Christabel looked after him, making a face. When she turned round again, she was surprised at the shrewd half-smile on James's mouth.

"Since he won't tell you why you're such a remarkable woman," said James, "shall I?"

"Please do."

"It's because you don't fuss."

"Fuss?"

22

"Yes. Most women of your age do nothing but fuss."

"Thank you."

"It's always, 'Do this,' or 'Do that,' and, 'Have you seen to this?' or, 'You must see to that,' about a thousand little things that don't matter a hoot. Always in a stew. They never do anything themselves. But they never stop worrying everybody else."

Christabel looked dismal.

"And I thought it was my girlish figure," she said—not above a spot of coquetry which was completely lost on the one-track-minded Mr. James.

"No, no. Not that," he assured her. "Though you've got a figure in a million. You remind me of Betty. Where is Betty, by the way?"

"According to Eleanor, she's with that friend of yours." Christabel's eyes narrowed. "He *is* a friend of yours, isn't he?"

"Nick Wood? Good Lord, yes."

"An old friend?"

"We were at school together. He always rather admired me, though I say it who shouldn't. Nick wanted to be a fast bowler, and couldn't bowl for toffee."

"Look out!" interrupted a sharp voice from the next room. "You'll slice your finger off!"

Again Christabel turned, so that she could see the dining room and the sideboard against its left-hand wall.

The narrow light over the El Greco shone down on Dwight, on Buller Naseby, and on Eleanor between them. In the middle of the sideboard stood a heavy silver bowl piled high with fruit. Eleanor had arranged a line of tumblers on the sideboard and poured brandy with the care of a chemist. If her father would not drink, she insisted, he must follow his eat-fruit-and-keep-fit fetish by having an apple. Flinging Buller Naseby aside, she squared her shoulders, picked up the fruit-knife, and began to peel the apple.

What happened then could not be distinctly seen. Dwight Stanhope let out an exclamation. The apple, trailing scarlet rind, flew one way. The fruit-knife flew another way. And Mr. Naseby began to swear.

"Somebody joggled my arm!" cried Eleanor.

"It's got blood on it," said Dwight, contemplating the knife on the floor.

"Nonsense!" said Mr. Naseby crisply. "That's a bit of apple-peel. Here."

He bent down and picked up the fruit-knife. It was a narrow, wafer-thin blade, longer than is usual in such knives, and very

23

sharp. They saw it gleam in flat silver against the carpet, before Naseby caught it up and put it back in the fruit bowl.

"All this fuss," giggled Eleanor, "about a little blood!" She put her forefinger in her mouth. "Anyway, it didn't cut me."

Christabel did not speak for some time.

"You were saying?" Vincent James prompted.

"Oh!" She woke up. "Yes. About your friend Mr. Wood."

"Rotten bad bowler," Mr. James offered helpfully.

"No doubt. Can you think of any reason why he should have been ransacking my husband's room earlier tonight?"

The other stared at her.

"Are you serious?"

"I don't *know* he was," returned Christabel. "I can't *prove* he was. But Hamley, who valets for Dwight, saw him coming out of Dwight's room. He said he'd mistaken it for his own room. That's absurd, because he's up there—" she nodded towards the ceiling—"and we're at the other side of the house."

"Still . . ."

"Incidentally, your Mr. Wood wouldn't have anybody valet for him. Wouldn't even have his things laid out. Kept his bag locked."

"Nothing in that," declared the other, though he looked a little shocked. "Lots of people do it."

"Oh, I'm probably imagining things! Or, if we must come to it, being fussy."

"Nick Wood," said James, with a crushing and unconscious arrogance which awed her, "is not a wrong 'un. At least, he wasn't when I knew him. I'll have a word with him. I'll ask him—"

"For heaven's sake, no!"

"Then what would you like?"

Christabel threw back her head and laughed. "Nothing. But you might keep an eye on him. I've given you the room next to his. You see, I don't really think there's anything wrong . . ."

"No, dear lady," said James with unexpected gallantry, "I think you're rather enjoying it."

As he spoke, Eleanor returned to the drawing room with the determined precision of a ballet dancer, carrying a tray of glasses with the effect of balancing it. Dwight, his hands in his pockets, followed behind a glowering Naseby.

Simultaneously, Betty Stanhope and Nicholas Wood entered from the main hall.

And, in the distance, a church clock struck the half hour after eleven.

24

4

The burglar did not attempt to break into the house until a quarter past three.

According to the almanac, the moon would set at half-past three. Dying and deathly, it now threw frozen radiance round the home which was known on notepaper as Waldemere, but which Flavia Venner had called Masque House.

A big house. Square, uncompromising, with a little octagonal tower at each of the two front corners, it was built of smooth gray stone blocks. Today we call this architecture Victorian Gothic, because roof and towers are crusted with sham battlements. Above them rose a sloping attic and a cupola topped by a flag staff. In front, a park of staunch trees and a tall iron-railed fence shut it away from the road to Tunbridge Wells. At the back, three floors of windows reflected the moon with frosty glitter.

The burglar looked at his wrist-watch.

Almost time.

Against the immensity of the hills, this house was nothing. In its own grounds, you could almost say its own puddle, it called aggressively for attention. At one side rose the cold bubble of the conservatory, iron and glass with an arched roof. Behind it stretched the flower garden, now only brown humps stiff with frost and desolation. Three steps—they were too shallow to be called a terrace—led down into the croquet lawn. Striking across it, lifeless on patches of frost, making a black wilderness of trees long petrified, that dead light rested on unresponsive windows: it was like the moon lighting up the moon.

The church clock, stiff through all its wiry weights, clanged out the quarter-hour. And the burglar moved towards the back of the house.

On his left-hand side, there was a wooden-floored porch outside the dining-room windows, formed by the overhang of the room above. He stopped to study it.

Of his face, you could see nothing except a black blob of cloth, with holes cut in it for the eyes. A shapeless heavy cap was pulled low round his ears. An equally shapeless coat and trousers, muffler, gloves, and tennis shoes, made a nondescript figure of him.

But he was cold. The night air numbed him; it searched out joints in that thin clothing, and pinched. As he breathed, the mask moved in and out; his breath smoked through and under it. Perhaps the moonlight, together with the clumsy eye-holes in the mask, prevented him from noticing the light coating of frost on the porch-floor. Perhaps he did not care.

In any case, the ribbed rubber soles of his shoes left footprints in the frost.

These dining-room windows were French windows only by courtesy. They were those full-length affairs commonly found in Victorian houses: stretching to the floor, but built like sash-windows. First the burglar took two short strips of adhesive tape, stuck to a roll of the same material in his pocket, and fastened them to one window below the junction of the two sashes. He glanced behind him, to make sure that the means of escape were still there. Then, with a very modern glass-cutter
. . .

Careful!

The glass-cutter crunched against that pane like a dentist's drill in a tooth. It seemed to rattle his own bones with its noise. He stopped dead, listening.

Still nothing.

Two minutes more, and he had sliced out a neat semi-circle of glass just below the window-catch. The adhesive tape prevented it from falling. He slid his gloved hand through the hole, unfastening the stiff catch. The window rolled up, not without a squeak. Thus, in the hour of suicides and bad dreams, he entered Masque House.

"I *ought* to know where it is."

He said this under his breath.

Pushing aside heavy velvet curtains, he slid through into the dining room and let the curtains fall. Warm air, quiet air, air that seemed as dark as the room inself, closed round him and made him shudder in the aftermath of cold.

Electric torch, now.

He took it out of his pocket and sent the tiny beam roving across the room. It passed over thick carpet, brushed against an oak-paneled wall, and found the sideboard. It found the massive service of silver plate, found the bowl of fruit in the center, and ascended to the painting that hung above.

"So!" he said.

El Greco, who saved his fingers from the Inquisition, had called that picture *The Pool*. Its harsh, arid colors were those of the tropics: Mexico, say, or South America. It contained those wizened figures and effects, struck with spiteful red and gold, which seem to have been made by storm or lightning.

But the man in the mask did not notice what it portrayed. He knew that well enough already.

Stepping quietly over to the sideboard, he propped the torch against a silver gravy-boat in such a way that it should shine up on the picture. Stretching, he carefully lifted down *The Pool* from its nail. It was not more than three feet wide by two feet high, but cumbersome in its heavy frame. As he lowered it, its edge struck the fruit bowl. A sharp little fruit-knife bounced out and rattled on the sideboard, followed by a rolling orange.

For God's sake, take care!

But the burglar was growing more confident now: as why not? He had, after all, little to fear. He paid no more attention to the fruit-knife. Instead he took out his own pen-knife, whetted for just this purpose. With careful fingers, the fingers of a man who knows the value of an artist's work, he set about separating frame from canvas.

The clumsy mask irked him, but he decided against taking it off. His gloves were less of an encumbrance. He had almost completed his work when, somewhere across the dining room, a board creaked.

The burglar twitched up his head.

He was facing the sideboard, crouched over. Where the light of the torch touched it, his face was a shapeless black blob except for the living, cryptic entity of the eyes: the eyes that shifted and shone as he turned his head.

He turned his head still further. He wanted to say, "Who's here?" Automatically he shut up the clasp-knife and dropped it into his pocket. But nothing happened. After an eternity he turned back again, his gloved hands on the loosened canvas.

This was the point at which someone came softly towards him from behind.

The burglar had no sixth sense which smelt murder.

5

In his bedroom upstairs, Nicholas Wood heard the crash.

Throughout the foregoing events, he had been lying in bed in a cold half-doze: wondering what his host really wanted, wondering what the game was, wondering whether he ought to be awake or asleep.

With his right ear dug into the pillow, he heard the church clock chime three. With his left ear emerging, he heard it chime three-fifteen. From that time he drifted into a floating doze— and was roused from it by such a noise as seemed to shake the house.

If heavy pieces of metal had been flung down on the floor they must have made a noise very much like that.

He sat up straight in bed. For a moment he could not remember where he was. His wits scattered like a jigsaw puzzle torn apart. A draught was blowing through the dark bedroom and the cold air woke him. Sliding his feet out from under the covers, he reached over for the chain of the bedside lamp. His watch on the bedside table, when he could focus his eyesight well enough to read it, gave the time as twenty-eight minutes past three.

"Oi!" called a voice. "Oi!"

From the adjoining bedroom, through the open doors of the bathroom between, he heard bedsprings creak and the sound of another lamp turned on.

"I say!" called the voice. "Nick!"

"Yes?"

"Did you hear something funny?"

"Yes."

He found his slippers and dragged on a dressing gown. At the sound of that voice his mind slid back over the years, to school. He remembered Vincent James, the great man of the sixth form. He remembered the voice—testy, faintly selfish—bidding him fetch something. He could have predicted what the next words would be.

"Go and see what it is, can't you?"

He reached the bedroom door as Vincent James, tying on a blue wool dressing gown over his pyjamas, came stumbling through the bathroom.

The passage outside was dimly lighted. At Waldemere, they kept a light burning in the main hall all night. Nick's room was near the rear end of the passage, on the left-hand side as you faced front. He walked forward into the main hall and listened.

Opinions differed as to whether this main hall had been Flavia Venner's effort to reproduce, in miniature, that of the Villa Borghese at Rome or the Opera at Paris. Bronze and marble and mosaic entwined it. On two sides of a gallery, marble balustrades terminated in a broad flight of carpeted stairs to the hall below. Seeing it in the light of the Triton lamps on the newel posts, he had a feeling that he was still dreaming.

But he was not dreaming.

"What are *you* doing here?" asked a woman's voice.

He whirled round.

Christabel Stanhope had come out on the landing from the opposite side of the house. She wore a fur coat, hastily drawn

28

n, over nightgown and negligée. Her silver-touched hair fell ound her shoulders.

"I was warned," he said.

"Warned?" She turned her head, and he could see the faint wrinkles round her neck.

"By Mr. James. That noise came from downstairs. From the dining room, I think. Excuse me."

He ran down the carpeted stairs. In the lower hall, the heels of his slippers clacked on the marble mosaic. He glanced past the doors on the left-hand side. Front room: morning room. Middle room: drawing room, where they had been sitting last night. Rear room: dining room.

He turned the knob of the door, threw it open, and with instinctive caution stood to one side. Nothing came out.

Groping inside the door, he found and pressed two electric switches. . . .

"That's done it!" said Nicholas Wood.

The word for it, perhaps, was ruin. A man with a black cloth mask covering his face, a shapeless cap pulled down on his ears, ancient clothes, muffler, and tennis shoes, lay on his back beside the sideboard. His gloved hands were thrown wide, his legs lay sprawl.

He had been stabbed through the chest. Blood soaked the old tweed coat and shirt, and splashed the corduroy trousers. Beside him was a crumpled canvas, the paint now broken and starred with cracks, cut nearly out of its frame. Around him lay a wreck and litter of silver plate, knocked off the almost denuded sideboard. The fruit-bowl had been spilled, too. Oranges, apples, and a hothouse pear strewed the carpet. The burglar's side still rested against a crushed bunch of grapes.

Nick's eye took in these details. He noted the blood-stained fruit-knife flung down on the carpet near the burglar's left leg. He now heard no sound except the ticking of the watch on the dead man's wrist.

Dead man?

Yes. Nick felt for a pulse at the wrist, and there was no pulse. He walked slowly round the room, finding that one window was open behind its heavy curtains. He made another circuit of the room, thinking very hard. . . .

Then he went out into the hall and closed the door.

Vincent James, his close-curling fair hair tousled, trailed along the hall looking sleepy and angry and aimless. He had a poker in his hand.

"Look here, Vince," his friend said. "Can I trust you?"

The other stopped short.

29

"Can *you* trust *me?*" he repeated, with a very curious inflection. He opened one eye, and half closed the other. "Can *you* trust *me?*"

"Yes."

"Well, by George! Considering what's been happening in this house . . ."

"Vince, I'm a police officer."

James slowly lowered the poker as though he were trying to balance it on the floor. He put his hand inside the breast of his dressing gown, and blinked. Prepared for this, Nick took from his own pocket the wallet that contained his warrant card, and thrust it out.

"Criminal Investigation Department, Metropolitan Police," James read. "Name, Nicholas H. Wood. Rank: Detective-Inspector, first class." After each of these items he would look at his companion, and draw his eyebrows together as though something hurt him. "Height, five feet ten inches. Weight, twelve stone. Hair, black. Eyes, gray. Distinguishing . . . Well, I'm damned!"

"*Sh-h-h!*"

"But what would they want you in the police force for? You used to be one of these literary blokes. What the hell good would you be in the police force?"

Nick took back the warrant card.

"And, anyway, what are you doing here?"

"I haven't got time to explain that now, Vince. See me later. The point is—" he gestured towards the dining room—"there's a burglar in there."

"Ho?" said James, catching up the poker again.

"The burglar's dead. He's been stabbed."

"Jolly good job. Who did it?"

"I don't know."

"But, hang it all," protested James, "you've got a right to kill a burglar. Shouldn't have *stabbed* him, myself. But still—if somebody breaks in, and you shoot him or cosh him, that's all right. Why don't you know who did it?"

Nick gestured him to silence.

Christabel Stanhope moved swiftly along the hall. That marble shell, with gilt Cupids along the cornices, now muttered to other echoes. It was as though you heard, very far away, a dormitory roused. Nick remembered that there were twenty servants in the house.

"I heard what you said." Christabel moistened her lips. "It's true? About your being a policeman?"

"Yes, Mrs. Stanhope."

30

"Then you're not . . . never mind." She started to laugh, but checked herself. "Did my husband ask you to come here?"

"Yes."

"Why?"

"Later, please. Where is Mr. Stanhope now?"

"I don't know. He's not in his room. You don't suppose *he* went off the deep end and killed . . . ?" Christabel put up her hands and ran them through the silky, fleecy brown hair that was touched in waves of gray. It was a gesture of conscious or unconscious grace. She spoke flatly. "A dead man in our house. How extraordinary. I've sometimes wondered what it would be like if something dreadful happened here; but it isn't anything like what I'd thought. Can we see what happened?"

"Yes. This way."

James, as curious as herself, opened the door.

Nick was keeping his own counsel, thinking his own thoughts, never taking his eyes from Christabel.

"The burglar was evidently having a try for the El Greco," he explained. "He got it down off the wall, and something happened."

"Why anybody should want to pinch one of these pictures beats me," said James, uneasily bellicose. "I don't know anything about art, but I know what I like. There's rather a lot of blood on him, isn't there?"

"Yes."

"Is the blighter dead? Are you sure?"

"Yes."

At first Christabel had stopped in the doorway, shrinking. Then she took a few steps forward.

"I don't understand this," said James, shifting the poker to his left hand. "It's the rummiest damn burglary I ever heard of."

"Agreed."

"If somebody killed the chap, why doesn't somebody up and say so? Hold on! Isn't that the fruit-knife off the sideboard? There? By his foot?"

"Looks like it."

"Well," argued James, "maybe he did it himself. If I remember, that knife was sticking in the bowl or somewhere. Suppose he started to take the picture, and slipped or something, and landed on the knife, and pulled all the silverware with him. That was the noise we heard, anyway. If he happened to slip and fall on the knife . . ."

"After which the knife pulled itself out of the wound and dropped on the floor?" said Nick.

"I forgot you were a detective," the other almost sneered.

31

This grievance seemed to have bitten deep into his soul. "A fat lot of good *you'll* be, young Nick!"

Christabel Stanhope spoke suddenly and loudly.

"Take off his mask," she said.

"Pardon?"

"Take off his mask," Christabel almost screamed.

With the door standing wide open, a draught from the open window caused the thick crimson-velvet curtains, under their gold-edged valences and tassels, to bell out with the weight and massiveness of sails.

The dining room was paneled to the ceiling in oak. Its refectory table and chairs, spoil of a Spanish monastery, set off the three remaining paintings. Velasquez's *Charles IV,* one of several such portraits, hung above the fireplace. At one side was Murillo's smoky *Calvary,* and at the other Goya's *The Young Witch.* Opposite them, against the right-hand wall as you faced front, was the sideboard and its ruin.

"Ah!" said Nick. "So you think so too, Mrs. Stanhope?"

"Think what?" cried Christabel.

Nick went towards the body, stepping carefully to avoid fruit and silver. As he did so, a padding of slippered footsteps sounded along the hall outside.

Larkin, a middle-aged butler with a conscience, appeared in the doorway. If the slippers might be disregarded, he was fully dressed except for his collar. Behind him were two more men in dressing gowns.

"Is everything all right, madam?" he asked.

"It's all right, yes," James snapped. "Go on back to bed. We've snaffled a burglar, that's all."

"Yes, sir. But I thought I heard . . ."

Larkin broke off.

Kneeling beside the body, Nicholas Wood gently eased back the peak of the cap, pulling it backwards and removing it. The mask was a piece of black muslin, with oval holes cut for eyes, fastened to the head with a home-made elastic. Nick pulled up the mask from below, disengaging the elastic from the ears. Thick, close-cut gray hair sprang from under it. The burglar's head lolled over until his face almost touched the lid of a silver vegetable dish.

Nobody spoke.

The thin, bloodless features showed even now qualities of mildness underlaid by strength. Strength above all. It was shown, in repose, by the very framework of the face. This was not a man you would have liked for an enemy.

32

Nobody spoke, that is, until Christabel went down on her knees by the body, and uttered an animal kind of scream.

Larkin, the butler, entered quietly and closed the door against his two companions.

The burglar was Dwight Stanhope—stabbed with a fruit-knife while attempting to rob his own house.

6

Larkin was the first to speak.

"Sir," he murmured, plucking at Vincent James's sleeve, "I think he's alive."

"Be quiet!"

"Sir," insisted Larkin, "I think he's breathing."

Nick, half disbelieving words that seemed to come out of nowhere, swung round. "Hold on! What was that?"

With a word of apology, Larkin began to edge sideways. He bent down gingerly until his face was close to Christabel's, and pointed. Dwight Stanhope's head had lolled over until his lips almost touched the cover of the vegetable dish. Against the polished silver showed a faint clouded spot: a trickle of breath through the lungs, so thin and uncertain as not even to show in the pulse, but still there.

"So it missed the heart!" said Nick. "And if it missed his heart . . ."

"Yes, sir. He may have a chance."

"Is there a doctor near here?"

"Yes, sir. Dr. Clements."

"Ring him up, then. Tell him—"

"We could send a car for him, sir?"

"Good idea. Do that."

Larkin suddenly remembered himself, and straightened up. "With your permission, madam?"

Christabel made a fierce gesture, implying that he might do what he liked. She now resembled a sort of handsome hag. She sat back on her heels, the fur coat billowing; and, so that she should not tumble over backwards, Nick took her gently by the shoulders and brought her to her feet.

"Just one moment," he said.

As Larkin left the room, he followed and—with the door closed—gave Larkin some rapid, low-voiced instructions which appeared to surprise the butler a good deal. Then he returned, to meet Christabel's face.

33

"Mr. Wood. Is he going to . . . ?"

"With any luck, Mrs. Stanhope, he may pull through."

"But you said he was dead!"

"Yes," jeered Vince, "you said he was dead."

Nick held hard to his self-control. One, two, three, he counted, four, five, six . . .

"I'm sorry, Mrs. Stanhope. It's the sort of mistake anybody but a doctor might make, and often does."

"You're not going to leave him lying there?"

"Sorry; it's all I can do. Besides, it would probably be more dangerous to move him now than to leave him where he is. It will only be a few minutes, until the doctor gets here. You see that?"

"Yes. I suppose so."

Nick glanced over his shoulder. "Vince, would you like to go upstairs and get dressed? This may take us the rest of the night."

His companion hesitated. Mr. James still had his hand inside his dressing gown like Napoleon; his red forehead and angry eye indicated that he resented such orders, however spoken. But this dissolved in fundamental good-nature.

"Right you are, old boy. At your service."

"Now, Mrs. Stanhope. Will you come with me, please?"

Christabel burst out: "Couldn't we just—*stay* here with him?"

"If you like. But I think it would distress you less if we went to another room. Next door, if you'd prefer it. You see, I'm afraid I have some questions I must ask you."

"Oh. Very well."

Instructing Rogers, who served as one of the foot-men-cum-valets, to stand guard at the dining room, he followed Christabel into the drawing room. Here he turned on a standard lamp by the fireplace. The arch between the two rooms could be cut off by enormous sliding doors, like prison doors, concealed in the wall. He pulled them shut with a soft, ponderous shock.

The fire had collapsed to red coals among ash. But central heating kept a ghost of warmth even at this hour of the morning when vitality is lowest.

Nick took up a leather box.

"Cigarette, Mrs. Stanhope?"

"Thank you," said Christabel, sitting down.

"Light?"

"Thank you."

"A while ago, Mrs. Stanhope, you asked me how I came to be here. I'm going to be frank with you, because I want you to be frank with me."

34

"Yes?"

He was not afraid of a breakdown on her part, of hysterics or even tears. That might come. But, if it did, it would come later. This, he judged, was the phase of shock. Christabel held her cigarette clumsily between the third and fourth fingers; each time she lifted it to her mouth, the hand half shielded her face. Her slack expression approached a smile. Her hair mingled with the sand color of the heavy sable coat, and little lines were etched round her mouth and eyes.

"I think you told us," he continued, "that your husband hated fancy dress?"

"Yes."

"Yet for some reason he decided to put on a fancy dress tonight."

"Yes." She sat up. "Do you know—I hadn't thought of that? It's funny, isn't it?"

"I've been told that Mr. Stanhope always had a practical reason for everything he did."

"Always!"

"This wouldn't be his idea of a joke?"

"Good heavens, no! Dwight rather dislikes jokes, except the kind you hear at a music hall. He especially dislikes practical jokes. He says that they humiliate people, and that the person who enjoys humiliating people is no better than a sadist."

"I see. Then can you suggest any reason why he should have tried to rob his own house?"

"No."

"You don't know anything about his business, for instance?"

"No. He would never tell me anything. He says a woman's business is to . . ."

"Yes?"

"To look pretty, and be charming," smiled Christabel. Her body grew tense, and her eyes nearly overflowed. Yet the paralysis of shock remained. While it held her like an opiate, her mind still seemed to be feverishly seeking the answer to the same bewildering question.

"Let's take tonight, Mrs. Stanhope. What time did you go to bed?"

Christabel lifted the cigarette again. "Why, the same time as you and the rest of us did. Twelve-thirty or thereabouts."

"Do you and Mr. Stanhope sleep in the same room?"

"No."

"Next door to each other, then?"

"No. My bedroom is at the front of the house, on the other side." She pointed. "It was Flavia Venner's bedroom. Then

35

there's a sitting room—what Flavia called her boudoir—and then a dressing room that we share, and then Dwight's bedroom."

"I see. Did you by any chance happen to hear him leave his room?"

"No."

"Or leave the house?"

"No," said Christabel. She paused. Her arched, plucked eyebrows drew down. "Leave the *house*, did you say?"

"Yes. Look here. A section of glass in one of the dining-room windows was cut out, rather neatly, from outside. Of course, that doesn't necessarily mean anything. He could just have raised the window, and stepped outside long enough to cut the glass. But, if this 'burglary' was planned as artistically as I think it was . . . why are you smiling?"

" 'Artistically' is a funny word to hear from a detective," said Christabel.

Nick shut his jaws. "I think we're going to find, Mrs. Stanhope, that this was an artistic kind of crime—on both sides. If it was done up right, I repeat, your husband probably went clear out of the house; fooled about the garden, maybe; and left clear traces which should later convince us that this was an outside job."

Christabel did not reply.

"What woke you, Mrs. Stanhope?"

"Woke me?"

"You were in the upstairs hall when I came out of my room at close on three-thirty. Do you mind telling me what you were doing there?"

"I—I don't really know."

"Did you hear a noise, for instance?"

"What noise?"

"Any noise."

Christabel shook her head. She hesitated. Then an honest, homely, whimsical expression crossed her face, and she looked up.

"If you really want to know the answer to that, I'll tell you. It was a dream. I dreamed that you—yes, you!—were a master-criminal, a sort of super Raffles or Arsene Lupin. Probably it was something that had been said before we went to bed, or those stories in the papers. Only it got mixed up with some talk of Eleanor's about murder. And all sorts of dreadful things began happening in the dream. Do you understand?"

"Go on."

"Well! I woke up in the dark, and I admit I was frightened.

36

You know how dreams can stick to you. So I went through to Dwight's bedroom. He wasn't there. His bed hadn't been slept in, even. By that time I wasn't frightened: only curious and a little bit worried. I came out into the hall. That's all."

She threw her cigarette into the fireplace, brushing ash down the sable coat.

"Do you think it was a premonition?" she added. "All that time, Dwight . . . !"

"Steady, Mrs. Stanhope!"

"I'm quite all right. Only—you promised to be frank with me, and you haven't been. What was Dwight doing, Mr. Wood?"

(That question, he thought, is more difficult than even you can imagine.)

"I'll tell you," he answered, "and then maybe you can tell me. Last Tuesday, the day after Boxing Day, Mr. Stanhope paid us a call. He's a friend of one of the Assistant Commissioners."

"One of the Assistant Commissioners?" asked Christabel, with inhuman calm. "Is there more than one? There's never more than one in the detective stories."

Nick was patient.

"As a matter of fact, there are five. But there's only one for the Criminal Investigation Department, if that's what you mean. Mr. Stanhope's friend is Major Stearns: Traffic. He was also armed with a letter from a very big wig at the War Office, named Sir Henry Merrivale. Major Stearns passed him on to Superintendent Glover, and Glover passed him on to Chief Inspector Masters, my immediate superior."

"Well?"

"Your husband," continued Nick, "then proceeded to tell one of the fishiest stories I've ever heard. He said . . ."

"Listen!" interposed Christabel.

The cry, whether of surprise or fright, had come from the hall outside. It was not loud. If it had not been for the thinness of the night silence, a taut sounding drum, they might not have heard it at all.

Nick went to the door, and opened it. After one glance outside, he stepped into the hall and closed the door. He experienced again the feeling that he had gone into a Victorian melodrama, and could not get out again.

The hall, quiet to ghostliness, rose up to its paneled dome. On two sides, the marble balustrades of the gallery closed it in at the height of the floor above. Dusky cut-glass lamps, borne by bronze Tritons on the newel posts, lighted the gray carpet of the marble staircase; they lighted the waste of the floor, circle and diamond mosaics of red and blue and gold; they drew a cold shimmer from pillars in the dusk. And—at the foot of the staircase—Betty Stanhope was lying still.

That was what completed the picture.

Betty was breathing: he could see that. Her eyes were closed. She lay partly on her side, and partly on her back, limply. Her fur-trimmed dressing robe was open. Her nightgown rucked and wrinkled by the fall against the lowest step, had slipped slantwise above her knees. One of her slippers had come off, and lay near her left foot. All this the dim yellow light brought out.

He walked across to her. Her face was nearly as white as the balustrade, her breathing thin.

"S-ss-t!" whispered a voice above his head.

Nick swung round rather wildly, and peered into corners before he located the source of the voice. It came from the landing of the staircase above. In the gloom he could just make out the face of a small girl, perhaps fifteen or sixteen years old. She was evidently kneeling there, peering round the corner of a pillar.

"S-ss-t!" said the voice.

"Yes?"

"She's fainted," the voice continued in an elaborate, hacking whisper. "She's been like that maybe fifteen minutes."

By instinct Nick started to reply in a whisper. But he corrected himself, coughed, and spoke out strongly.

"Then why the devil haven't you done something about it?"

"Me go down there?" demanded the voice, rising a little. "When there's a murderer loose? Besides, the Old Boy told us not to."

"What old boy?"

"*Him*. And besides," added the voice, using a clinching argument, "I'm not dressed."

"Yes, but, damn it all, *I* don't know what to do! What happened to her?"

His informant edged a little further round the pillar.

On closer inspection, he thought he recognized the eager, freckled little face as that of one of the maids he had seen whisking through the house. The voice spoke with romantic relish.

"It was that Mr. James."

"What?"

"Oh, he didn't *do* nothing to her! He came out of the dining room maybe fifteen minutes ago . . ."

"Yes?"

"And started up the stairs. Miss Betty was coming down. She

38

said, 'What's happened?' And he took hold of her hands and said, 'It's your father.' Those was his exact words. 'It's your father,' he said. 'He dressed up as a burglar, and somebody stabbed him; but don't worry; they think maybe he won't die.'"

The small girl gulped. She was now on all fours, definitely showing her face round the pillar.

"What'd he mean by that, sir?"

"Never mind. For the love of Mike, can't you come down here? There's nothing to be afraid of."

The small girl ignored this.

"It didn't seem to bother Miss Betty just then. Mr. James, he went on up to his room. And she walked down till she'd got to the bottom step. Then she stopped, and muttered-like, and then sort of scrunched up like a dish-rag and fell over on the floor." The voice grew wistful. "She's awful pretty."

Yes; and that was the trouble.

He had announced that he did not know what to do, which was a lie. Such first-aid is elementary. He was too conscious of Betty's physical presence. Still it had to be done.

"If you'll show me which is her room," he said, "I'll get her upstairs."

"All right. But you won't tell the Old Boy I spoke to you, will you?"

"Who is this Old Boy, anyway?"

"*Him.* Old Larkin. Mr. Larkin."

"Oh! No, I won't tell him. Let's go."

Bending down, he put his arms under Betty's shoulders and knees, and picked her up. She was lighter than he had anticipated. Unobtrusively he took the opportunity to shake down the wrinkled nightgown.

"Incidentally," he added, balancing her and taking one step up, "who was it that cried out or shouted out in the hall here a few minutes ago? I heard it in the other room. That was what brought me out."

"Oh, that was Miss Eleanor."

"So? I didn't know she was awake."

"Oh, yes, sir. It was when they were putting poor Mr. Stanhope in the lift—so's not to jolt him, I reckon—and taking him upstairs to put him to bed. The lift's at the back of the hall. I didn't *see* it. But they were carrying him on a camp-bed for a stretcher; and I reckon they must have bumped him against the lift-door, so Miss Eleanor . . ."

Nick stopped dead.

Terrified by the expression on his face, the small girl ducked

39

back behind the pillar. It was several seconds before she could risk one eye again.

"Just one moment," he said clearly. "Repeat that. Are you telling me that somebody has moved Mr. Stanhope before the doctor can get here to see him?"

He received no answer. The front door at Masque House—double doors in a box-like vestibule walled with colored glass—faced the world outside with an iron knocker shaped like a lion's head. Somebody began to bang this knocker, with metallic, thudding blows which reverberated up under the dome.

It put the small girl to flight. He had a brief glimpse of a braided pigtail flying, of heels kicking up the legs of red-striped pyjamas, as she scuttled along the gallery towards the top floor and safety.

And Eleanor Stanhope, whom he had not been able to see because the height of the great staircase had intervened, walked across with rapid strides towards the front door.

7

"Come in, Dr. Clements," invited Eleanor.

Opening the inner glass doors of the vestibule, she unbolted and unchained the outer ones, dragging them open after a scuffle with a doormat which got in the way.

She did not look at Nick and his burden on the stairs. She was now wearing brown slacks and a yellow knitted jumper with a high neck.

"Sorry to have routed you out at this hour." she continued, dragging the doctor's overcoat back over his shoulders so that he writhed as though imprisoned, "but I'm afraid it's serious."

"Not at all, not at all," said Dr. Clements, still writhing. He was a shortish, stout man with a close-cut gray beard and mustache, who breathed noisily. "My dear young lady! Allow me!"

Larkin—still collarless—had miraculously appeared. Dr. Clements extricated himself from his overcoat, handed coat and hat to Larkin, and picked up his medicine case.

"Oh, ah. Very well. Where is he?"

"Upstairs, in his bedroom. You know the way."

Still breathing noisily, the doctor crossed the hall. Brushing past Nick, he paused only long enough to direct a glance at Betty and contort his face into an expression of sympathy.

"Poor girl!" he said, touching her hair. "Better put her
40

down," he added, to Nick. "Her eyes are open. The blood'll go to her head."

Rather hastily Nick stepped down to floor level and set Betty on her feet, steadying her. Eleanor watched them in gloom, her hands on her hips.

"Please!" muttered Betty, pushing him away.

"Are you all right? Can you stand up?"

"Yes. I'm fine." Betty gave a convulsive shudder, and pressed the palms of her hands over her eyes. "I must have keeled over or something. I'm sorry."

"Come and sit down. Would you like some brandy?"

"No, thanks."

"But *I* should," said Eleanor.

This was bravado. He turned towards her. Eleanor saw the thunder cloud coming; she clenched her fists and inflated her chest in a sort of weak-kneed defiance. For she was shakily sober, emptily sober, and the shadows under her brown eyes emphasized the luminousness of the whites.

"Now don't you pitch into me!" she said. "I don't care *who* Vince James says you are. I wasn't going to leave him lying there—" moisture, perhaps partly of nerves, started to her eyes—"all over blood, and looking like that."

"Would you mind telling me how you managed it? I gave strict orders . . ."

"Larkin didn't know. He was at the phone. I persuaded Rogers and Hamley to do it. We walked on tiptoe, and you couldn't hear us because the double doors were closed between. After all, what did we do? All we did was take him upstairs, and undress him, and put him to bed. And wash him up a bit." '

"You realize that, if your father dies of a hemorrhage from being moved, you'll be partly responsible?"

"And you can't scare me, either!" But the tawny complexion had gone white. "Betty, pet, support me!"

"Also—if he does die—you've probably destroyed the evidences that would tell who killed him?"

Eleanor brushed this aside.

"I won't think about that," she said. "That doesn't matter. Because he's not going to die. I thought you looked a good sport. I certainly tried to be a good sport to you and Betty last night, if you know what I mean. But no. No! You come charging in here and look jail at everybody instead. If you could see anybody *you're* fond of, lying there, with the draught blowing on him and not a ghost of color in his face, and *you* wouldn't move him . . . well, you're too damn cold-blooded to live, that's all."

41

Nick drew a weary breath.

"All right," he said. "Forget it. We'll see what we can do as matters stand."

"You mean that?"

"Yes. It's no good arguing against such an idiotic line. So forget it. What did you do with his clothes?"

"Whose clothes?"

"Your father's. The fancy-dress outfit."

Eleanor's glance of inquiry was evidently a signal to draw Larkin again from some mysterious retreat.

"I'm sorry, sir. If I had been there when they did it—"

"Never mind. Clothes? Shoes? You didn't take anything out of the pockets, did you?"

The butler was emphatic.

"No, sir. The clothes are locked up in the wardrobe in Mr. Stanhope's dressing room. Three of us can testify that they haven't been interfered with in any way."

"Good. Then if you two—" he turned to Eleanor and Betty—"wouldn't mind going into the drawing room with your mother, and waiting for a minute, I want a word with the doctor."

"You'll let us know?"

"Yes. In you go."

Throughout this, Betty had not spoken a word. The more mercurial Eleanor put an arm round her waist and guided her. The brown-gold head and the dark one disappeared. Larkin coughed.

"If you'd like me to take you to Mr. Stanhope's room?"

"Not for a minute. I want to get some clothes on. If the doctor finishes before I do, give me a shout."

"Yes, sir. About that information you asked me to get—"

"Later."

"Very good, sir."

Now if (argued Nicholas Wood) if I could get out of my head the notion that this whole thing is a Victorian melodrama, the going might be easier. Yet, even so, even as a period-piece, there is something wrong with it. That, however, is not evidence. So let us consider the evidence.

Pondering it, he trudged upstairs. He glanced across the gallery when he reached the landing. The fourth door from the front—on the opposite side—stood ajar. That would be Dwight's bedroom. Nick walked down to his own bedroom in the passage.

He had reached that light-headed state of tiredness when voices seem to hum inside the skull like tuning forks. His

42

bedroom, done in the Napoleonic style of the First Empire, made a satiny pattern of stripes and squares. He had left his windows closed, feeling that there was enough cold air in the house as it stood. His watch, on the bedside table, gave the time as ten minutes to five.

He put on trousers and a sports coat over his pyjamas. Going into the very modern bathroom adjoining, he examined his face in the mirror. Chin looking a bit blue, but shaving could wait until morning. He swilled out the reddish sediment at the bottom of the washbowl, brushed his teeth, and sloshed his face in cold water.

"For, consider!" He spoke aloud to his image in the mirror. "We have here . . ."

"What's that, old boy?" inquired Vincent James, sticking his head out of the next room.

"Nothing. I was talking to myself. It's a bad habit. Did you tell Eleanor Stanhope what had happened?"

Vince, in a heavy white cricket sweater and flannels, came in and sat on the edge of the tub.

"Yes. I went in and woke her up. Thought I'd better." He hesitated. "Hanged if she didn't hurl her arms round my neck and address me as Pinkey. Who's Pinkey?"

Nick searched his mind.

"If I remember rightly, there's a certain Commander Dawson—whoever he is—that she once called Pinkey."

"*That* bloke?" Though Vince's vanity was offended, a great relief showed in his eyes. "Well, I wish him luck. But Eleanor was upset, right enough. Practically before I'd finished telling her, she slung on some clothes and tore downstairs in the lift. Damned embarrassing, you know. I say, Nick. The other one is very attractive, isn't she? The younger one."

"Betty?"

Vince nodded. In the mirror, Nick studied the reflection of his companion's heavy, handsome face.

"Never mind that, now," Vince added, slapping his knees. "We can—er—deal with such recreations in our spare time." He grinned. "How's the old man?"

"I don't know. The doctor's here. We ought to have a report any time now."

A discreet tap at the bedroom door, in fact, announced the arrival of Dr. Clements. Firmly shutting the bathroom door against his highly offended friend, Nick went to answer it. The stout little doctor was divided between a hushed portentousness of manner, and a very real worry.

"Inspector Wood?"

"Yes. How is he?"

Dr. Clements evidently considered it bad policy to answer a direct question. He kept shaking his head like a china figure.

"These internal-bleeding cases," he confided, "are the very devil. Tell me. What was the nature of the weapon employed?"

"We think it was a fruit-knife."

"Ah! A very thin blade? I thought so. The lips of the wound were so compressed that I could scarcely find it. Not—unusual. But difficult. Yes. Very difficult."

"Is he going to live?"

Dr. Clements pursed up his lips.

"I should say—well, yes, perhaps. A seventy-thirty chance, at least. The lungs were not touched. Of course, the question of the knife-thrust is complicated by his other injuries."

"Other injuries?"

"My dear sir! Surely you noticed?" Discomfort racked the stout figure. "No, perhaps not. Circulation was at a minimum and the marks would be slow in forming." He paused. "Someone, with the most extraordinary brutality, seems to have leaped or stamped on Mr. Stanhope as he lay on the floor. Three of his ribs are broken, and he is fortunate to have escaped concussion."

"Leaped or stamped on . . . ?"

"His body and head."

Nick felt physically cold. Across the room he could hear his watch ticking on the table.

"Hatred," he said.

"I beg your pardon?"

"Hatred," repeated Nick, staring at the somber puzzle. "The missing element." He swept this aside. "Tell me, Doctor. Mr. Stanhope was attacked. There was a struggle, during which he was stabbed and the silver was knocked off the sideboard. Could these extra injuries have occurred in the course of the struggle?"

"No, sir," returned the doctor with formal courtesy. "At least, not in my opinion. It was calculated violence against a man who could not help himself."

Nick faced it.

"Is there any means of telling the *sort* of person who did it? I mean . . ."

"I know what you mean," said Dr. Clements. His eye grew evasive. He stroked at his close-cut gray beard. A cloud of unhappiness surrounded him. But he was honest. "I should say that the injuries were inflicted by a small man—" he paused —"or a woman."

44

There seemed to be no comment to make. Hatred, the missing element.

"Thank you, Doctor. You're staying on?"

"Yes. I shall be with the patient, if you want me." Still the doctor lingered, his hand on the knob of the door. "Excuse me, but what is your standing here?"

"Officially, I haven't any."

Dr. Clements's face fell.

"My profession," he said, "entails certain disagreeable duties. I am obliged, ordinarily, to report such things as this to the local police." His eyes opened. "Unless, of course, you can assure me that Mr. Stanhope was hurt—well!—by accident, in the course of some Christmas charade, or the like? That's what Larkin gave me to understand, over the telephone."

"You needn't report it, Doctor. I'll accept the responsibility."

"Thank you," said Dr. Clements. "Thank you very much. How pleasant it is, sometimes, to know one's self for a liar!"

And he bustled out.

There were now certain things to be done. Downstairs, in the drawing room, three women waited for news. They would have to know the truth now, touching more matters than they were prepared for.

In the drawing room, when Nick opened the door, nobody spoke; but three faces were turned towards him. Somebody had made up the fire. Eleanor, in her brown slacks and yellow jumper, stood by the fire and chain-smoked. Christabel leaned back in the easy chair, her long legs crossed. At some distance from them, Betty sat bolt upright on a sofa, the fur-trimmed robe pulled round her; only her eyes seemed alive, and they watched Christabel.

"It's all right," said Nick. "The doctor says he's got a good chance of pulling through."

There was a silence while you might have counted five.

"Thank God!" murmured Christabel.

With self-controlled emotion, Eleanor dropped her cigarette on the hearthstone and stamped on it. Betty said nothing, but she expelled her breath.

"Oughtn't we to go and sit with him?" asked Eleanor. "Or get a nurse or something? When will he be conscious enough to tell what happened?"

"The doctor will do whatever is necessary. In the meantime—"

"In the meantime," volunteered Christabel, "we still want to know why he did it, don't we?"

45

"*I* can tell you why he did it," said Betty.

Christabel looked surprised.

"Betty, dear—" she began mildly. It was only too clear that she regarded her own daughter as the baby of the family, an attitude which Betty's self-effacing manners did much to confirm.

"Let's talk about it, please," said Betty, shifting in her seat with faint impatience. "Mr. Wood's been thinking about it all the time. Mr. Naseby as good as came out flat and said it. Father's in trouble, isn't he? Money trouble."

"Rot!" exploded Eleanor, with hollow incredulity.

Christabel looked uncomfortable. "Do you really think you ought to talk about such things, my dear?" she asked, as though Betty had mentioned some particularly unsavory family scandal.

"We've had an easy time of it," said Betty. "We're a terribly useless lot, I'm afraid. But that's how he liked to see us, or at least mother and Eleanor. So he'd never say anything if things got difficult."

Betty turned to Nick.

"The aggregate value of those four paintings in there," she nodded towards the dining room, "is well over a hundred thousand pounds. I know, because somebody wanted to exhibit them at the World's Fair in New York next year; and he refused.

"You could sell them. But you couldn't get anything remotely approaching their value nowadays. Sir Charles Lytle says that paintings have been a drug on the market since Munich. So what could you do? Naturally, they'd be heavily insured. You could stage a fake burglary and 'steal' them. By that you'd first collect the insurance, and secondly sell them on the quiet to some private collector like Nelson or Van Dymm . . ."

Christabel sat up.

"Betty Stanhope! Are you accusing Dwight of—"

"Mother, please!" urged Betty. She got up and went across to Christabel. "It surely doesn't surprise you as much as all that, does it?"

"I don't believe it," said Eleanor flatly. The brown eyes swung round. "And anyway, if it *is* true, why have you got to go and blurt it out in front of a Scotland Yard man?"

Betty made a face.

"I'm sorry. But there's no harm done. And it's better than believing he went out of his mind, isn't it? What other earthly explanation can there be? He's the most practical man that ever lived. He never had an idea that wasn't practical. Yet he dresses

46

up in a mask and does all these weird things: why? To get the insurance, because he wanted to take care of us. That's the obvious explanation, isn't it?"

"Yes," interposed Nick. "That's the obvious explanation."

He drew a deep breath. All three women, who had caught the change of tone, were now looking at him. Betty's hand tightened on Christabel's shoulder.

"So I think I ought to tell you," he added, "that it's not the true explanation."

8

Eleanor spoke sharply.

"Wait a minute," she said. "Who's loony now?"

"I'm beginning to think I am. As your sister says, that's the explanation you'd think of first off. I believed it myself, until yesterday afternoon. Only—it won't work."

"But why not?" demanded Eleanor, now apparently arguing on the other side. Christabel's foot had begun to tap on the floor. Though both of them had scouted Betty's suggestion, it seemed clear that both secretly believed it.

"I'll tell you," he replied. "I'd started to tell Mrs. Stanhope a while ago, only we were interrupted.

"Last Tuesday Mr. Stanhope came to the office and had a talk with Chief Inspector Masters. He said he had reason to believe an attempt would be made to burgle his home and steal at least one of his pictures; and he asked for a police officer to be sent down here over the week-end, posing as a guest.

"The chief inspector, naturally, wanted to know how he knew all this. Mr. Stanhope firmly refused to give any details. At that point, ordinarily, he'd have been just as firmly shown the door. But there were several reasons why he got close attention.

"First of all, we smelt funny business. It's an old trick. When an amateur crook—excuse me—plans the burglary-for-insurance swindle, it's ten to one he first goes to the police and says he's afraid he'll be robbed. He thinks it puts the police off the track, whereas actually it's what starts suspicion going. Like the anonymous-letter ramp, you see. When there's a plague of anonymous letters, you can bet your shirt that the person who is being most consistently and foully abused by 'em is the very person, usually a woman, who's writing the letters."

He paused.

47

The faces of his listeners wore a very curious expression.

"Now, the chief inspector was worried. Mr. Stanhope's a great power in the land. We'd had orders from Higher Up to treat him well and give him anything he wanted within reason. Masters said—and you'd better know this—'My lad, that gentleman's up to funny business, and it'll be a hell of a how-de-do if we have to run him in for it.'

"They finally decided to send me down here, just as Mr. Stanhope asked. My orders were to keep an eye on him. If he tried it on, I was to interfere and choke it off *without* scandal. In the meantime, we were to investigate Mr. Dwight Stanhope's position, and see how he stood."

Nick paused again. He took a few steps backwards and forwards in front of the fire.

"Yes?" prompted Christabel.

"I'll not deny—" he hesitated—"that there was another reason for my being sent here. The chief doesn't neglect any bets. But we won't go into that reason now. It's not very likely to affect any member of his family.

"Well, we thought we had Mr. Stanhope's game taped. That is, until we learned the facts." Nick stopped on the hearth-rug. *"Not one of those paintings,"* he added, *"is insured for as much as a penny."*

It took some time for his hearers to assimilate this. Eleanor opened her mouth as though to speak, but thought better of it. Betty's hand fell from her mother's shoulder. Christabel's face wore a bothered frown which showed her real age.

"Not insured?" she repeated.

"Correct. And I'll tell you something else. Mr. Stanhope is not hard up. On the contrary. His credit has never stood higher, and he made his biggest killing—financial killing—less than a month ago."

"Thank the Lord for that," muttered Eleanor, rubbing the back of her hand across her forehead.

Christabel cried out. "Then in heaven's name," she said, "what was Dwight up to?"

"You," said Nick, "tell *me.*"

He gave a parody of a shrug. "Now look here," he went on, after a pause, "I don't say Mr. Stanhope is ten times madder than a March hare. I'm pretty sure he isn't. He strikes me as being a man who knows his own mind, and does things for a good reason."

"Correct," nodded Betty.

"But what reason? Why does he stage this hocus-pocus of masks and glass-cutters and the rest of it? He hadn't a penny to gain from it. You tell me he's not in the habit of playing jokes. I've been frank with you because somewhere, in somebody's mind, there must be an explanation."

"Not in mine," returned Eleanor, shaking her head. "But you could ask him, couldn't you?"

"Yes. If he recovers."

"Don't *say* that!" Eleanor stamped her foot. She was wearing red open-work sandals, and the small shallow heel rattled on the hearthstone.

"Yes. After all," said Christabel, "if the knife didn't reach his heart, and Dr. Clements says he's going to get well . . ."

"It wasn't only the knife-thrust," he said with careful deliberation. "There are other injuries too."

"What other injuries?" Betty asked quickly.

He ignored this.

"You see the position," he continued, himself whetting a knife for them, and preparing to turn it in their emotions. "This attack on Mr. Stanhope wasn't an accident. That's to say, somebody didn't mistake him for a real burglar, and attack him under that misconception.

"There are two reasons why that's so unlikely as to be nearly impossible. First, the attacker would have had no reason to conceal it afterwards. A masked burglar breaks in; you don't know who he is; you tackle him; and in the row he cops one. You then sing out and announce your capture. Don't you?"

"I really can't say," shivered Christabel. "*I* should never tackle a burglar, masked or otherwise."

"I might," observed Eleanor, putting her hands on her hips with a swaggering gesture. "That is, if I had a weapon of some kind." Her eyes clouded. "No, I'm a liar! I'd yell for Vince or Pinky Dawson. But I like to *think* I might."

Nick disregarded this.

"Second, there's the question of the savage personal attack on Mr. Stanhope. When he'd been stabbed, and was lying helpless on the floor, somebody stamped on or beat his body and head in such a way that three ribs are broken and he just escaped concussion of the brain. That was an ugly bit of work. Personal hatred. Blind, savage escapism."

Smoothly, without appearing to notice the current of horror which struck his listeners and held them like a charged wire, he went on to explain.

"There's only one conclusion we can come to. Somebody knew that Mr. Stanhope—for whatever reason—was going to dress up as a burglar. Somebody was waiting for him. Somebody—"

"Stop," interrupted Christabel: not loudly, but in such a compelling tone that he obeyed. "Need you play this game of cat-and-mouse with us?"

"Madam, somebody is playing cat-and-mouse with me. My job is to find out who. And I mean to do it."

He was tired. He still had a problem that made no sense. His words rang with harsh clearness in the Doges' room, under the pink-mottled marble.

Most of all he was conscious of Betty. With every hour, almost with every word—or so he imagined—he was alienating her still more. He told himself that he didn't care. Long ago Masters had warned him against taking a personal interest in anyone while he was on a job. "You're never a guest, my lad; and you're not even a human being. People don't consult us before they decide to rob a till or cut a throat; so why consult them?"

Unfortunately, he remained a human being. Betty was neither a worldly-wise woman like Christabel, nor a sort of amiable and sensual tomboy like Eleanor. She suited him; he could think of no other word. It was Betty who said quietly:

"Please. Let's not lose our tempers. That *is* true, is it? About someone wanting to—hurt him?"

"Someone did hurt him. Badly."

"But why?" asked Christabel, as though the personal injury had been to herself. She shaded her eyes with her hand. "Why? He's the most harmless person in the world."

"Not to his enemies, I shouldn't think," said Betty.

"No, and I shouldn't think so either," said Eleanor. "He's a good hater, like every other person who's worth a damn in this world. Only he's civilized enough not to let it be seen. So if somebody wanted to hit back at him . . ."

Nick interposed. "That's exactly what I mean. That's where I need help. Why should he have dressed up like that? What was he trying to prove? Who were his enemies?"

Betty's alert, swift-slapping intelligence caught him up here.

"That wasn't what you said. You said that somebody was 'waiting for him.'"

"Yes. Well?"

"Now you seem to be talking about business enemies. But, when you first mentioned it, you sounded as though you might be talking about somebody here. In this house, even." Her blue eyes were fixed steadily on his. "Were you?"

"If you don't mind, Miss Stanhope, I'll ask the questions."

Betty's eyebrows went up. "Just as you like," she agreed in a

50

small, impersonal voice. But she turned away, and would not look at him.

"Were you talking about somebody here?" demanded Eleanor.

"Of course not, my dear," soothed Christabel, evidently not concerned. "The idea is too fantastic even for this place. Isn't it, Mr. Wood?"

(None of them, he noted, even seemed to think seriously about this suggestion.)

"He was talking about people who mightn't have liked Dwight," Christabel pursued. "I can't help there; because, as I say, he never told me anything. Though, come to think of it, he did have a bad business quarrel with one of his best friends. Not that there's anything in that, I'm afraid."

"He *is* going to get well, isn't he?" asked Eleanor. "That's all I want to know. He *is* going to get well?"

"We'll hope so."

"Oh, I can't stand this!" said Eleanor explosively. After staring back at Nick for a moment, she drew in her breath with an air of decision, and strode towards the dining room. Christabel spoke on her usual mild note.

"Where are you going, my dear?"

"I'm going to get a drink," returned Eleanor, rolling back the double doors to the dining room, and turning round. "Then, I'm going to sleep. I wish I could sleep for a week. It's all very well for you, Bet. He isn't your father; and, anyway, you read books and live in a dream most of the time. It's not so bad for Christabel, even, as it is for me."

Nick was after her instantly. "Don't touch the top of that sideboard!"

"I wasn't going to touch the top of the sideboard. The decanter's in the cupboard underneath it. Or at least that's where it was."

"If you've got to have the decanter, Miss Stanhope, I'll get it. Stand over here, please."

Instinctively both Christabel and Betty followed. All four stood in the archway, surveying the wreck beyond. The litter of fallen silver and fruit made strong colors against a thick black carpet. Crushed grapes marked the position of what had been Dwight Stanhope's side. Nick reflected with at least some satisfaction that he could sketch that position pretty well from memory.

Propped against the sideboard, hanging loose from its frame, that cracked El Greco looked as though somebody had set a

51

heavy foot on it. Nick noted something else. Where Dwight had been lying—hitherto concealed by his body—was a small nickel electric torch. The stained fruit-knife had not been moved.

"Just one moment," he requested.

He took a pencil from his pocket and laid it on the carpet to mark the position of the fruit-knife. Then, using only the tip of a finger at each end, he picked up the knife carefully and carried it to the dining-room table, where he put it down.

Eleanor tried to speak with cynical flippancy.

"Aren't you going to wrap it up in a handkerchief to preserve fingerprints?"

"Anyone who was fatheaded enough to do that," he said, "would only mess up whatever fingerprints there might be. Will you stand to one side, please?"

Next he put down his fountain pen to mark the position of the electric torch. Though the torch was more difficult to balance against two finger-tips, he carried it across to the table and laid it beside the knife. Not much more to do here, he decided. Eleanor's (doubtless well-meant) efforts had already done enough to the evidence.

He opened the door of the sideboard, found a depleted decanter of brandy, and held it out.

"Here you are," he said. "Anything else I can do for you, Miss Stanhope?"

Eleanor made no move to take it. On the contrary, she had backed away until she was standing just under an illuminated picture across the room. It was Goya's *The Young Witch*. Bold of line and satiric of design, it was not a painting you would have hung in any house where there were young children.

"You're rather horrible," Eleanor flung at him. "After all, you might remember you're our guest."

"I do remember it. Otherwise—"

"What?"

"Let it go. Don't you want the brandy?"

"No, I don't," returned Eleanor, never of the same mind for ten minutes running. "I want to know what happened here."

While they had been speaking, Betty slipped across to the draught-swayed curtains of the left-hand window. She raised them and peered beyond. She even got inside the embrasure, letting the curtains fall after her, before she came out again.

"Hullo!" she observed, holding back the curtain. "It's begun to snow."

"Has it, dear?" asked Christabel without interest. "I shouldn't touch anything, if I were you."

Betty hesitated. At length, as though making up her mind,

she consented to address Nick. "You're in charge," she said. "You've made it clear you don't want any interference. Still, it might interest you to look outside this window."

He went over to the window, and held the heavy curtains aside with both hands. Bright light from the dining room streamed out on a small porch, formed by the overhang of the room upstairs. Even so, the light was now quite bright enough.

The window had been raised from the bottom as high as it would go. Searching after a box of matches in his pocket, Nick found one, struck it, leaned out, and held the match high. Its flame burnt clearly in cold, almost windless air.

Beyond the porch, large damp snowflakes were falling slowly. The porch itself, protected, was white with a frosty rime now thawing. It would crackle underfoot. In the coating he could see several footprints or the parts of footprints: their pattern was the ridged pattern of Dwight Stanhope's tennis shoes. All of them pointed inwards, towards the window.

"Well?" inquired Nick.

"Did *he* make them?" Betty wanted to know.

"Undoubtedly. You remember, he was wearing . . . but then you didn't see him, did you?"

"No, no, of course not! What I mean is, it's even more elaborate than we thought, isn't it? He must have gone clear outside the house before he came in again."

Christabel spoke wearily. "My dear, that's nothing new. Mr. Wood suggested it hours ago. What if it does mean he went outside the house?"

Nick blew out the match and dropped the curtains. He must get a tracing of those marks before the thaw set in. Meantime, he looked straight into Betty's eyes. He asked her a question without words, and she answered it.

"You see what else it means, don't you?" asked Betty, answering him by speaking to Christabel.

"No, dear, I can't say I do."

"Mother, please! Those are the only footprints on the porch, aren't they?"

Christabel came gracefully over to see for herself. Even after she had drawn the curtains and looked out, she did not appear to be much enlightened.

"It's very late, Betty, and I'm tired. Playing detective is all very well in books and games; in fact, it's fun; but when you try it in a dreadful thing like this . . ."

"It means," said Betty clearly, "that nobody followed him in."

But she did not, or could not, give the real answer.

53

9

At two o'clock on the following afternoon, a dusky day white with snow, Nicholas Wood came down the main staircase intent on a walk in the open air.

The rest of the household were still in bed. But signs of life must shortly be evident, since he passed a maid carrying a breakfast tray up to Christabel's room. Though he had had only a couple of hours' sleep himself, he felt amazingly refreshed. His evidence was collected, and he had been on the telephone to Chief Inspector Masters at Whitehall 1212.

In the lower hall, now brightly lighted by a cornice of concealed bulbs, he found Larkin. The butler looked doubtful, and perhaps he had reason. Just inside the front door stood a very large trunk and an even larger packing-case. Across both had been painted, in gaudy red-and-white letters, the words THE GREAT KAFOOZALUM, with such additional labels as "This side up," and "Handle with care."

Nick stopped short, drawing on his overcoat.

"Good morning, sir," said Larkin.

"Good morning."

"I hope your breakfast was satisfactory?"

"Yes. Very," replied Nick, with only a hazy idea of what he had eaten.

"And—Mr. Stanhope, sir?"

"He's resting easily. One of your blokes sat up with him all night. The doctor ought to be back soon." Nick pointed to the cases. "Incidentally, who or what is The Great Kafoozalum?"

The shadow of a smile crossed Larkin's face.

"He's the magician, sir."

"Magician? What magician?"

"I don't know whether you were told? It's our custom, every New Year's, to give an entertainment for the children. Under the circumstances, I hardly think it'll be given this year. But Mr. Stanhope booked this conjuror, who's the latest thing at the Palladium. The Carter Paterson people just brought these."

"Oh," said Nick, repressing a lively curiosity about the trappings of hocus-pocus. "Well, I'm going for a walk. I'll be back in time to see Dr. Clements."

"Very good, sir. Excuse me . . ."

"Yes?"

"That information you asked me to get last night." Larkin lowered his voice. "Do you still want it, or shall I forget it?"

"No; I'm afraid *I* forgot it. What did you find out?"

Larkin became still more conspiratorial.

"The front door was bolted and chained on the inside. You probably noticed that yourself, sir, when Miss Eleanor opened it for Dr. Clements. The door to the conservatory was locked and bolted. The back door—that is to say, the area door below-stairs, leading to the kitchen—was also locked and bolted."

"And those are the only ways into the house?"

"Yes, sir."

"What about downstairs windows?"

"All fastened on the inside."

"So!" muttered Nick.

He digested this while Larkin helped him into his coat and opened the front door. He descended the front steps into a dim, silver-lit world muffled with snow. And on the slope of the lawn, scuffling her feet in the snow, stood Betty Stanhope.

Betty made a not-very-Victorian figure. She had put on what used to be called a skiing-suit. From booted trousers to peaked hood, it was a dark wine-color against snow and black trees. Framed by the hood, her face had color from the cold, and her eyes looked brighter; a pink nose was nevertheless a handsome nose. She waved a wool glove at him.

"Imagine meeting you here," said Betty, scuffling across to the steps.

"I was just going for a walk."

"So was I. Would you care to come with me?"

"There's nothing," declared Nick, "I should like better. You must know the roads. Which way?"

She eyed him. "The best one—" she nodded towards the back of the house—"is over the fields there. But the snow's rather deep."

"Never mind. I've got galoshes on."

This statement was a piece of undue optimism.

So much he admitted to himself before they had gone three hundred yards, and his brisk, confident step sank his legs nearly to the calf in damp adhesive snow. In such circumstances, however, no man worthy of his salt will acknowledge any discomfort.

They plowed ahead in silence. Five minutes more, and the house was left some distance behind. Whether or not because of a release from the atmosphere of Waldemere, he felt his spirits lighten and his whole outlook change.

"Are you *sure* you're not getting wet?" persisted Betty.

55

"Not a bit of it!" He stepped into a hidden pot-hole as far as the knee, and righted himself. "You seem all dressed for a snowball-fight, though."

"Shades of St. Moritz," said Betty. "That's all this is good for, as a rule. We were to have gone there after New Year's, only—"

"Only what?"

"Well, Eleanor threw a tantrum because Vince James wouldn't go. He wanted to go somewhere else. So we decided not to go to St. Moritz."

"Tell me. Do you ever go into a tantrum?"

"It wouldn't do me any good if I did," Betty said seriously. "They'd only say it was liver and dose me with something. I know. I've tried it."

"Then tell me something else. What do you think of Vince James?"

Betty gave this careful consideration, while they trudged across the slope of a field.

"He's awfully attractive . . ."

"Yes?"

"I can't blame Eleanor, really . . ."

"No?"

"But I do think, between ourselves, that he's a most dreadful pain in the neck."

Now it does not, as an ordinary thing, cause intense pleasure to hear a friend of yours called a pain in the neck. Had anybody but Betty said this, Nick would have argued the point. To Vince's good qualities—his honesty, his straightforwardness, his skill at games—Nick paid tribute. But certain casual remarks of Vince's last night had worried him more than he cared to admit.

In sheer exuberance he bent down and scooped up a handful of snow. His hands fashioned it, automatically, into a snowball. Betty was looking at him in a puzzled way, her breath smoking in the air as she laughed. They had come out into a level stretch, dim under the lead-covered sky, where a snow-covered stone wall loomed ahead at about the height of a man's waist. Nick's jubilant eye, roving round the landscape, alighted on an object which appeared to be resting just on or beyond the crest of the wall.

It was a top-hat.

"Well, well, well!" said Nick.

There is something about the combination of a top-hat and a snowball which arouses the best desires—or, if you prefer, the worst—in all public-spirited persons.

To be just, it never occurred to Nick that the hat belonged to anybody. It could not possibly have belonged to anybody. It was a top-hat of great age, such as might have been scorned by a tramp or even a Zulu chief. It was such a hat as could be used only for decorating a snow-man. In that uncertain light, it seemed to him that it did decorate a snow-man which children had built on the other side of the wall.

Betty read his thought. Bending down, she scooped up snow and kneaded it.

"I'll bet I can hit it before you do," she challenged.

"Done!" said Nick. He balanced on his right foot, set himself, and threw like a rifle-bullet.

It was deadly aiming. The hat, struck squarely amidships, took flight like a bird. turned over twice in the air, and disappeared into a snowdrift. Nick breathed on his half-frozen hands as Betty launched her own missile. He had been prepared for this. He was not, however, prepared for what followed.

Up over the wall arose, in awful majesty, a face so terrifying in its wrath that at first glance it hardly appeared human.

"What the goddam holy blazes do you think you're doin'?" bellowed an irate voice.

They had a momentary glimpse of spectacles pulled down on a broad nose, and a bald head. The figure had just time to say this, but no more, before Betty's snowball—a rather squashy one—landed squarely in the center of its face.

After this, the figure did not say anything. You could see it breathe. It leaned thick arms on the snow-covered wall, as on a bar-counter, and appeared to be taking a reflective survey of the fields through crusted spectacles.

"My God," whispered Nick, "it's the old man!"

Betty spoke in a similar whisper. "What old man?"

"Sir Henry Merrivale."

"Not the War Office man?"

"Yes. He's a friend of your father. He sent your father to my chief inspector, and recommended all possible courtesy—"

Betty found her voice. "I say," she called, "I'm *terribly* sorry!"

A series of little shivers or twitches went over the large bulk of the man leaning on the wall. He wore an overcoat with an old-fashioned astrakhan collar, and had knitted mittens on his hands.

"So you're sorry, hey?" he breathed in a hoarse, husky voice, and cleared his throat. "You're sorry!"

"Yes! We couldn't see—"

"One of 'em," said H.M. dispassionately, "one of 'em lures me into lookin' up by knocking my hat off. And the other is

57

waitin' to cop me square in the mush when I do. And then they say they're sorry. Oh, Lord love a duck!"

Nick took a step forward. "It was thrown before you got up, sir! She wasn't trying to hit you. She was only aiming at your hat, just as I was."

H.M. turned slightly purple.

"I mean, we didn't know it was *your* hat. We thought it was only an old cast-off hat that didn't belong to anybody."

"Aren't you being rather tactless?" asked Betty under her breath.

"And anyway," insisted Nick, "what were you doing down on the other side of that wall?"

"I was readin' a map, damn you," said H.M., suddenly flourishing a large and much-creased expanse of paper which streamed out of a small book and fluttered like a flag. "For three mortal hours I've been trampin' these roads—where I could find 'em—trying to find a place called Masque House. And it's not on any map either. I was sittin' there as peaceful as you please, when a damn great piece of ice comes whizzin' out of nowhere . . ."

"But it's not really called Masque House," said Betty. "It's called Waldemere. You must have passed it half a dozen times."

"Thank'ee," said H.M. "That's really comfortin' news, that is."

"You see, we come from there."

"*You* come from there?"

"Yes. I'm Betty Stanhope."

Betty was really concerned. She stumbled forward, taking a handkerchief out of a pocket in her skiing suit.

"Let me wipe your face off," she urged coaxingly. "And Mr. Wood will find your hat. We honestly are most awfully sorry."

H.M. remained on his dignity. He assumed the lofty stoicism of a red Indian, his arms folded, while Betty leaned over the wall to swab down his face, remove and polish his big spectacles, and make a tentative dab at his bald head. Though he would not admit to being mollified, the corners of his broad mouth relaxed a little.

"This wench here," he conceded grudgingly, "is not without *some* feelin's of decency and respect for my gray hairs, anyway. But you—!"

Nick climbed over the wall and fished the great man's hat out of a snowdrift.

"Do you know Mr. Wood, Sir Henry?"

"Know him?" said H.M. "No. Not socially. I'm not speaking

58

to him, if that's what you mean. Thinkin' it's funny to hit people in the schnozzle with snowballs, at his age! Cor!"

"But he didn't do that, Sir Henry. I did."

H.M. always believed what he wished to believe.

"Never you mind who did it," he said darkly. "Just you gimme my hat . . . no, I'll have it from you; not from him . . . and then maybe I'll feel better."

"But how did you get here, sir?" demanded Nick. "Haven't you got a car?"

"Sure I got a car. As far as I know, it's still back in the snowdrift where I left it. This is my lucky day, this is."

Betty bit her lip. "If you've come to see my step-father on business, I'm afraid he's not in very good shape to be seen. There's been an accident."

H.M. looked uncomfortable.

"I know there has, my wench," he said. "Masters gave me the gist of it over the phone. That's why I'm here."

"You mean you've come to help us?"

"Well . . . now." H.M. looked still more uncomfortable. "Help's a big word. I'm here because I trust my common sense. Y'see—" here he glared at them—"Dwight Stanhope's one of the few really honest men I've ever met. I don't mean fair-to-middling honest, like most of us. I mean the real thing. He's not a fraud or a fake. One of his rulin' passions is a dislike of frauds and fakes. When he came to me first off, I could have told Masters he wouldn't be mixed up in any insurance swindle."

"We've already proved he wasn't," Nick pointed out. "Didn't the chief inspector tell you?"

H.M. seemed to have forgotten his grievance.

"Sure, sure. All the same, what's the position now?"

"With regard to what?"

"With regard to the police takin' action about all these high jinks last night."

"No action is to be taken until Mr. Stanhope recovers enough to ask for it. If he does."

"You mean, if he recovers?"

"No: I mean if he asks for it."

"So?" muttered H.M., giving him a very curious look from behind the big spectacles. "Masters thinks it may be like that, hey? And in the meantime?"

"Superintendent Glover rang through to Colonel Boyne, who's Chief Constable here. Their fingerprint man is being sent along to do what's necessary, unofficially, in case we need ammunition. As we're likely to."

"H'mf. So."

"But the whole point, sir, is this crazy business of a man robbing his own house. You're an expert in craziness . . ."

H.M. looked pleased.

"And if there's anybody in the world we should be glad to see here, it's you. What do you make of it?"

"I dunno, son. Masters did mention it. It's another of the things that sort of intrigued the old man's curiosity. He did it. But why did he do it? Oh, my eye."

"Can you think of any reasonable explanation?"

H.M. sniffed. He started to rub his nose with a mittened hand; but, finding the nose tender after the impact of the snowball, he squinted down it in a way that was hideous to behold, trying to assess the damage. This reminded him again of his grievance, and thunder clouds gathered.

"Do you think I've got nothing better to do," he roared, "than to stand about givin' advice at a time like this. Look at this beak of mine! It's swollen and inflamed. It needs attention. My feet are frozen stiff. I haven't had a bite to eat since early this morning . . ."

"You poor dear." said Betty—a term which, in strict justice, H.M.'s own mother could never have applied to him; but which Betty evidently believed. "I was forgetting!"

"Of course," agreed Nick. He eyed H.M.'s corporation. "Er—can you manage to climb over the wall?"

The insult, if entirely unintentional, was a deadly one. H.M. looked at him. For one mad moment he seemed to consider putting his hands on the wall and attempting to vault over it like Douglas Fairbanks. But his better judgment rejected this. He clambered across with dignity, and landed with a thud amid spurting snow.

"Good," said Betty. "Now come along straightaway. We'll take you to the house."

"No," said H.M.

"But don't you want to go?"

"Over two hours ago," said H.M., holding up the map, "I got mad. I swore a great oath that I was goin' to find this ruddy house all by myself. And I will. You just tell me where it is, and let me alone. I'm all right."

"But we were only out for a walk—!"

"You go on with your walk," glowered H.M. "I got some cogitatin' to do. I want to be alone. Which way?"

Betty glanced round helplessly.

"If you insist," replied Nick, pressing her arm, "keep straight head and you can't miss it. It's the big place with stories fifteen feet high and battlements round the top."

"And the house is yours," Betty called after him. "I'm sure they'll do everything possible to make you comfortable."

H.M. squinted round over his shoulder. "I hope so," he growled. "I hope so. G'by."

They watched him go down the shallow slope, stoop-shouldered, broad as a hogshead, the hat fixed firmly on his head and the map trailing from his hand. His grudging stride kicked up a spray of snow at every step.

"So that," murmured Betty, "is the criminals' nemesis."

"Yes. You wouldn't think he was such a crafty old devil, would you?"

"No, I certainly shouldn't. Is he?"

"Yes. He's the old man. But in private life he practically challenges you to take him seriously. Do you know what?"

"Well?"

"I've got a dirty, low-down impulse," said Nick, "to mold a juicy snowball and have another shot at his hat, just to see what he'd say."

As though warned by some telepathic instinct, H.M.—now twenty yards away—turned round and peered suspiciously over his shoulder. Betty was galvanized.

"For heaven's sake, no!"

"It's all right," he assured her. "I've got no intention of doing it. I only said I had the impulse. That's how he affects people. Do you follow me?"

Betty turned her head away. "No, certainly not! Well, yes, maybe. You seem a completely different person this morning, Mr. Wood."

"And so do you, Miss Stanhope. Is it the house, I wonder?"

"Please! Let's not talk about it."

Far away, past snow-candled trees in the bowl of the valley, they could just see the towers, cupola, and flag staff of Waldemere rising above its sham battlements. He watched it through the steam of his breath.

"You asked me when we were in the little theater," he reminded her, "whether I knew why it had been called Masque House. But you wouldn't explain why. In fact, there were several things you wouldn't explain. You seemed to have something on your mind. And then you fainted when you heard your step-father had been stabbed."

Betty was leaning against the stone wall. She gave him a brief glance, something of a pitying glance, round the corner of the

61

wine-colored hood. But she had no opportunity to comment, even if she had wished to.

Along the little lane behind them, winding between the stone wall on one side and a hedgerow on the other, sounded a faint padding noise overlaid by a rollicking, musical jingle.

"Ahoy there!" a voice hailed them. "Hoy!"

10

It was a small sleigh, the first Nick had seen in years, drawn by an excited horse apparently unused to such work. It contained two men. One was Buller Naseby, in a bowler hat, his overcoat collar turned up round his ears. The other, the driver, was a middle-sized, wiry young man in a blue reefer great-coat and naval cap. He waved a whip with manifest pride in the figure he cut, while the sleigh flew towards the curve beside the wall.

"Hoy!" he repeated. "Betty!"

Betty waved a hand in reply, and turned to Nick with real pleasure.

"It's Roy Dawson," she said. "Commander Dawson."

"Look out, you fool," rasped Mr. Naseby in his dry voice. "Do you want to upset us?"

Commander Dawson stood up in the sleigh, spilling a lap-rug which was clutched by Mr. Naseby.

"Hard your helm, blast you!" the driver was saying. "Hard-a-port: ease off a point: dead slow and stop. What's the matter with the ruddy horse?"

"How do you expect her to understand such talk?" asked Mr. Naseby. "Just say, 'Whoa!'"

"Whoa!" said the Commander obediently.

The horse decided to obey. Lurching dangerously, the sleigh skidded sideways, flinging glittering particles and clearing the lane like a snow-plow: it came to rest almost broadside against the wall. Commander Dawson, not at all discomposed, continued to stand up. His long, sharp-nosed, good-natured face glowed with pride. You could understand the reason for his nickname, since shining mahogany-colored hair showed under his cap.

"What do you think of my equipage?" he demanded. "Bought it, horse and all, in Tunbridge Wells. Every road hereabouts is impassable."

"But, Roy! We didn't think you could come!"

Commander Dawson seemed half in a dream.

"The old *Desperate* put in yesterday morning," he responded. "And here I am." His expression grew heavily diffident. "I thought Eleanor might like to go sleigh-riding. And the rest of you, of course. Er—how is she? And your mother? And the old man?"

Betty did not reply.

"If this weather holds, we can get in some skiing. And it's going to hold, if I'm any judge. Here, what's the matter? Is anything wrong?"

"This is Detective Inspector Wood," said Betty.

"Detective inspector, eh?" murmured Mr. Naseby.

Commander Dawson rather absently saluted him with the whip. His sandy eyebrows were pinched together over his long nose.

"The old man," continued Betty, with her eyes on the ground, "was stabbed last night. Yes, I said stabbed. That's not all. His ribs were broken and his face bashed about where somebody stamped on him."

Out of the darkening sky drifted one snowflake, and then another.

"Good God," breathed Commander Dawson.

"When did he die?" asked Mr. Naseby.

Nick intervened here. Touching Betty's arm as a signal, he studied the faces above.

"It happened during a burglary," he informed them.

"Good God," the Commander said again. "How is Eleanor taking it?"

"A burglary, eh?" repeated Mr. Naseby. He was shaken by a sort of cold-blooded excitement. "Didn't I tell him? Didn't I warn him? Didn't I say so, over and over again?"

"At some time just before half-past three in the morning, a burglar broke into the dining room and tried to steal one of the pictures."

"Which one?" asked Commander Dawson. "The Velasquez?"

"No, the El Greco."

"Ah. The gilded man," nodded Commander Dawson.

Nick had heard this term once before. He filed it away in his mind for future reference.

"But the burglar, oddly enough, turned out to be Mr. Stanhope himself," he added; and went on to give them a short but very thorough account of what had happened. "Finally, you'll be glad to hear that Mr. Stanhope isn't dead."

"Not dead?" frowned Mr. Naseby.

"No, sir; not dead. Why should you suppose he was?"

Mr. Naseby smiled a brief, skeptical, pouncing kind of smile.

"Because, young man, I didn't see how Dwight Stanhope could have survived an attack like that. I still don't. His bones, man! His bones!"

"What about his bones?"

"That's nothing!" interposed Betty.

"Oh, isn't it?" inquired Mr. Naseby. "You've seen Dwight Stanhope. Tall, strong-looking chap, you'd say. Yes. Well! So he is, in a way. Only he's got bones like glass. I've forgotten the medical term; but you've heard of it. Supposed to be a product of in-breeding."

"Really—" Betty began.

"He won't play games with a lot of running in 'em in case he falls down. That's why he got all those injuries last night. Well-known fact. Ask anybody. Ask his wife."

While they were speaking, another snowflake sifted down, and then another. One of them touched Commander Dawson's cheek. He put up his hand to it, startled. His intelligent, light eyes shifted under the peak of the cap.

"I don't understand this." He spoke slowly. "Which isn't very original. But it must be pretty rotten for Eleanor. This talk of in-breeding is a lot of rot." Then he woke up. "Look here, what are we driveling about? We're wasting time. Pile into the sleigh with us, you two, and I'll circle round to the main road."

"Is there room for all of us?" asked Betty.

"We'll make room. You can sit on somebody's lap."

She sat on Nick's lap. Commander Dawson cracked the whip, somewhat half-heartedly after his earlier exuberance. He joggled the reins on the horse's back, and they plodded off with slowly gathering speed. The tinkle of the sleigh-bells rattled.

"Damn silly, isn't it?" he said. "This sleigh, I mean. But it reminds me. When are you off to Switzerland?"

"We're not going," answered Betty. "Roy—Vince James is here."

"Look out, man!" screamed Mr. Naseby. "Mind that curve!"

"Sorry."

"Let your reins lie light. Haven't you ever driven a horse before?"

"No," said the Commander. "What were you saying, Betty?"

"Vince James is here."

"Oh. Good egg, James." He nodded. "I've got a present for Eleanor."

But he spoke no more until they reached the main road, and turned back towards Waldemere.

With some difficulty he eased the sleigh through the open gates in the tall iron-railed fence. They drove up through the park to the front of the house. Though an effort had been made to sweep the gravel drive, a hard crust of snow remained beneath and the sleigh moved with rather too much ease.

At the front steps, the drive branched right and left. Betty directed him towards the left: that is, the side that would have been the right if you had been facing towards the front. On this side a big iron-and-glass conservatory, a sort of Oriental bubble, was built out on a glass passage from the house. The drive curved past it.

"Bessie will be all right," said Betty. She sprang out and patted the horse. "Throw the blanket over her—if they gave you one?—and leave her here. I'll send McGovern out to see to her."

The falling snow had thickened. Masque House, the surface of its stone blocks unbroken by so much as a water pipe or a trail of ivy on that smooth gray face, loomed up in the dusk, shot with lights. And Commander Dawson hesitated.

"Do you think I'd better go in?"

"Why ever not?"

"Well, your mother can't be feeling any too keen. I don't want to barge in. If you could send Eleanor out to see me?"

"Nonsense! You're staying here, you know. Come along."

When Larkin admitted them, the rush of warm air made Nick conscious of his soaked shoes and trouser-legs: they felt as numb as though he were walking on stilts, and his hands ached.

Christabel Stanhope, a poised but subdued woman, was just coming downstairs. She stopped short.

"Why, Pinkey Dawson!"

"Hello, Mrs. Stanhope," said the Commander, with some diffidence. He removed his cap, showing a mop of mahogany-colored hair to which plastering with water had imparted a shine like a waxed table.

"What on earth are you doing here?"

"I came back in a sleigh," said the Commander.

"You came back from the Mediterranean in a sleigh?"

"No, ma'am. I mean—"

"Your hat and coat, sir?" said Larkin.

"Christ, yes!" said the Commander. "I mean, I beg your pardon!"

His hostess smiled. She knew exactly how to assume the right amount of motherly tolerance, at the same time indicating gently that she wasn't as old as all this.

"For heaven's sake, don't call me 'ma'am'! You can't imagine how it makes me feel. But you don't like to be called Pinkey either, and I don't blame you. Very well. You call me Christabel, and I'll call you Roy."

"Good enough," agreed the Commander. He added in a steadier and more grown-up tone: "I've heard all about it. It's a rotten business."

"Yes. Yes." Christabel refused to discuss this. "Eleanor *will* be glad to see you. Shall I call her?"

"Hadn't I better go to her instead?"

"If you like. I think she's in the billiard room."

Commander Dawson walked with elaborate unconcern across the marble floor. The billiard room was across the hall on the side opposite that which contained the morning room, the drawing room, and the dining room. As the Commander disappeared round the corner of the staircase, Betty stripped off her gloves and threw back the hood of her skiing suit from tousled hair.

"If he'd beat her!" whispered Betty. "If he'd only beat her!"

"Perhaps, my dear, or perhaps not. Do get those wet clothes off before you catch cold."

(Masque House was back again. Once more Betty seemed to grow anemic and colorless, in the rôle she had chosen to play.)

"The doctor's here," Christabel reported, touching an elaborately coiffured head which made waves of brown and silver. Not a line showed in her smooth face or round her broad mouth. "Dwight's better, though he isn't conscious yet. Hello, Mr. Naseby. Mr. Wood, there's a man here looking for you."

Nick felt warm with satisfaction.

"Sir Henry Merrivale? Good!"

"Sir Henry—" Christabel stopped. "What in the world do you mean? This is a young man with a mysterious manner. He's taking fingerprints."

"But H.M.—"

"That's Dwight's friend, isn't it? What about him?"

"He *is* here?"

"Not that I know of." Christabel stared at them. "And I haven't been out of the house all day."

"But, Mrs. Stanhope, he's got to be here! He started for here over half an hour ago! And he couldn't have lost the way. You could see the house from where we were standing."

"Have we had any visitors, Larkin?"

"No, madam." Larkin, moving away with the hats and coats, paused and assumed a very thoughtful expression. Once he seemed about to speak. But he shook his head.

66

"You see?"

Nick and Betty exchanged an uneasy glance.

"Do you think he changed his mind about coming here?" the latter suggested.

"When he felt like that? And when there's not another house for a half a mile? We'd better send out a search party. In the meantime: where is the man who's waiting for me?"

"In the dining room, I believe." Christabel turned over her hand and regarded the tips of the fingers as though she remembered a faintly distasteful experience. Her light blue eyes strayed towards Naseby. "I'm afraid I must go up to Dwight, Mr. Naseby. Please make yourself comfortable. Betty, dear, *are* you going to take off those wet things?"

"In a minute, mother!"

Nick hurried towards the dining room, and Betty instinctively followed him. The dining room would not now have pleased a conscientious housemaid. So many surfaces were smeared with "gray" powder that the place had a somewhat rakish look. At the big refectory table, under overhead lights, sat a long-jawed young man in a blue serge suit. Insufflator, brush, and camera lay beside him. Notebook and pen were under his hand. A series of small cards, like visiting-cards, were piled in front of him. He was contemplating the stained fruit-knife, but he got to his feet as Nick entered.

"Inspector Wood?"

"Yes?"

"I'm Smeaton, sir, from Maidenhead. I've got a lot of stuff for you; though I don't expect most of it'll be much good. Is it O.K. for the young lady to be present?"

Nick hesitated slightly. "Yes. Carry on."

"I don't know if you'll approve, Inspector. But I usually find it's the best policy to go straight to people and say, 'Do you mind if I take your fingerprints?' Saves time and trouble, if you're tactful. Nobody here made any difficulty about it."

"Yes?"

"Now, this knife." Smeaton picked it up. He took a strong lens from his pocket and examined both sides of the silver handle. "There are three sets of prints on it."

"Three sets?"

"Yes, sir. Overlaying each other. Also blurred, as though it'd been handled with fabric on top of 'em. One set I can't identify. One set belongs to Miss Stanhope, Miss Eleanor Stanhope. The third, the top set and clearest, belongs to Mr. Dwight Stanhope."

Smeaton put down the knife.

"By the way," he added. "Miss Stanhope volunteered something about that. Not that I asked her, mind! None of my business. Still, I thought you'd better have it."

"Right. Well?"

"Miss Stanhope said, 'Don't be surprised if you find my dabs on that knife.'" Smeaton consulted his notebook. "She explained that—at about half-past eleven last night—she was in here, and started to peel an apple for her father. Mr. Stanhope was with her, and a man named Mr. Naseby. She says somebody jogged her arm. The knife flew out of her hand, and fell on the floor. Mr. Naseby, she says, picked up the knife and put it back in the bowl."

Nick searched his mind.

"I can't say *I* remember the incident."

"May I speak?" volunteered Betty.

"Yes?"

"It's all right. That happened just before we—" Betty pushed back her smooth, soft, tangled hair, and color rose in her face—"before we came downstairs. Both mother and Eleanor mentioned it to me later."

"The point is, Inspector: How did Mr. Stanhope's prints come to be on the knife? Miss Stanhope swears blue that her father never touched that fruit-knife at any time."

"S-ss-t!" hissed a voice behind Nick.

By this time he should have been used to such voices, or at least to this particular voice. He recognized its peculiar timbre even before he turned round.

A small, snub-nosed, freckled countenance, with large eyes, was poked round the partly open door to the hall.

"Excuse me, sir," the small girl whispered, "but did you lose a gentleman?"

"Aren't you—" Betty began.

"I'm Lisa, miss." The small girl spoke with frank, admiring worship. "I'm the between-maid. But mostly they calls me Golly. Did you lose a gentleman?"

"Yes!" said Nick.

The small girl withdrew her head for a quick reconnaissance of the hall outside, and poked it back again.

"Was he a stout gentleman with big spectacles?" she inquired carefully.

"Yes!"

"Was he an awful angry-looking gentleman that wanted something to eat?"

68

"Yes!"

"You don't mean that he got here after all?" cried Betty.

"Please, miss: yes, he did."

"But where is he?"

"Please, miss: they put him in the servants' hall."

11

In the servants' hall," repeated Betty. Suddenly she opened her mouth in horror, and pressed the palms of her hands over it.

" 'The house is yours,' " quoted Nick, with his eye on a corner of the ceiling. " 'I'm sure they'll do everything possible to make you comfortable.' "

"My dear man, this isn't a joke!"

"Well, maybe not." He turned to the small girl. "How the devil did they happen to do that? No, don't run away! Nobody's going to hurt you. Come in and close the door."

The small girl did so.

"It was the Old Boy that did it," she explained, alluding to Larkin not without secret glee. Then she became preternaturally solemn again. "*I* could tell he was quality, even if the Old Boy couldn't."

"But what happened?" asked a bewildered Betty.

"Please, miss: he came and knocked at the front door. Mr. Larkin opened it. And he *was* wearing that funny old top-hat, and the fuzzy-collared coat like the pictures you see of people that used to be on the stage.

"Please, miss: Mr. Larkin said, 'Are you The Great Kafoozalum?' The stout gentleman sort of pulled his head back and kind of blinked at him, and said, 'Well, if you want to put it like that, I s'pose I am.' Mr. Larkin said, sharper-like, 'Are you the conjuror?' Then the stout gentleman sort of made a funny noise, and stuck out his chest—" Lisa was an expert mimic; they could almost see H.M. doing it—"and said, 'My good man, I'll have you understand I know more about conjuring than most anybody in England.' And Mr. Larkin said, 'Good; why couldn't you say so?' And marched him down to the servants' hall.

"And, please miss: that's how it happened."

The small girl stopped, out of breath.

Betty looked at Nick. "Come along," she said. "I'll show you the way."

"Right. Carry on, Smeaton. I'll be back in a minute. I always thought," he added, as they went out, "that the magician was a privileged person. Do you usually stick him in the servants' hall?"

"Good Lord, no! He's a guest. He's invited to come the day before the show, and stay all night. But Larkin must have thought this one looked *too* disreputable."

The servants' hall, together with the kitchen, was in the lofty basement. They went down a flight of stairs at the rear of the main hall beside the lift, and along a lighted passage towards a closed door at the front.

"Poor H.M.!" said Betty. "He must be feeling—"

"Is he? Listen to that!"

From behind the closed door issued a sudden vigorous burst of applause, evidently made by many hands. This was followed by the sound of H.M.'s bass voice, pitched in a strange, unnatural, high-falutin key.

"I thank you," it declared, with a modest, self-deprecatory cough. Then it said:

"With your kind permission, I will now attempt to entertain you with another small trick. This trick, I might say, was taught to me by the Grand Vizier of the Maharajah of Eysore, on the occasion of my visit to his palace while shootin' tigers in India."

"Can you do the Indian rope-trick?" demanded a voice.

"What's that?"

"I said, can you do the Indian rope-trick?"

"Certainly," affirmed H.M., with a rashness unmatched by any miracle-monger since the days of Dr. John Dee.

"Cor lumme! You can?"

"A bagatelle, sir. A mere bagatelle, I assure you."

"Let's see you do it, then!"

"Wot's a bagatelle?" inquired a keen, suspicious voice, not to be taken in.

"Sort of game. Where you roll balls up a board."

("I knew it," said Nick. "The old devil's having the time of his life.")

"I don't want to see him roll balls up a board. I want to see the Indian rope-trick."

"Looky here. I should be—hurrum!—only too pleased to oblige the funny-lookin' gentleman in the chauffeur's uniform. However, since unfortunately we've got no rope suitable . . ."

"Oh, yes, we have. There're those ropes hooked to the wall in the bedrooms, in case of fire. What about it?"

"Are you goin' to shut up and let me get on with this trick," said H.M., a note of very unprofessional pugnacity creeping into his tone, "or aren't you?"

70

And a woman's cold, authoritative voice, evidently that of the housekeeper, backed him up. It restored immediate silence.

"I should think so, indeed. If the magician wishes to entertain you by rolling balls up a board, please have the good manners to watch him and refrain from comment."

Betty softly opened the door.

In a long, large room, with a big clock on the wall and a cheerful fire in the grate, some dozen persons were gathered in absorbed attention round a long, scrubbed dining table. At the head of it stood H.M. A cleared plate and beer glass stood in front of him; his napkin was still stuck into his collar. But he manipulated his arms, mesmerically.

"With your kind permission, I will now attempt to entertain you with another small trick. This trick, I might say, was taught to me by the Grand Vizier of the Maharajah of Eysore, on the occasion of my visit to his palace while shootin' tigers in India. Has anybody got a pound-note?"

"Sir Henry," Betty called softly.

Her entrance caused a stir. Everybody instantly got up except the housekeeper, who gave her a gracious nod and rose with dignity after some thirty seconds.

"I think you're wanted upstairs," said Betty. "Do you mind?"

H.M.'s attitude was a mixture of truculence and sheepishness. He glowered at her over the spectacles pulled down on his broad nose.

"Well," he said, drawing the napkin out of his collar, "I expect I got to go. Thanks for the grub. Hoo-hoo, everybody."

The united and regretful chorus of farewell indicated a popularity which characterized H.M. in every public-house from Land's End to John o' Groat's.

Betty held open the door for him. As he stumped out, the watch-chain dangling across his corporation and making gold gleams against the shiny black suit, a number board on the wall buzzed sharply. All heads turned towards it, including H.M.'s.

Hamley, the footman who had been up all night in Dwight Stanhope's room, drew a deep breath.

"That's for me," he observed. "Mr. Stanhope again."

H.M. blinked at him. "You won't forget what I told you, son?"

"Got you, governor!" said Hamley, with a conspiratorial wink. "No, I won't forget. But he wouldn't have been left alone anyway. The London 'tec's already seen to that."

H.M. came out, and Betty closed the door.

"I was going to apologize," said Betty, clearly at a complete

71

loss what to make of him, "but now it doesn't seem to be necessary."

"Apologize? Burn me, no!" H.M. was gleeful. "I've been havin' a lovely time." He looked at Nick. "Also, I bet I now know as much about this attempted-murder business as you do. Or more."

Nick was enlightened.

"I see. So you deliberately kept from telling Larkin who you were?"

H.M. meditated.

"Well . . . now. I wouldn't say I ever did anything deliberately."

"Wouldn't you? *I* would."

"Only, if you can manage to get into the servants' hall under the right bona fides, you hear an awful lot. You hear much more than you ever would above-stairs. I heard all about the wounds. In fact, I heard something that startled the scalp off my head. It wants looking into, if it's true." The small, sharp little eyes fixed on Nick. "Son, this business is bad. It's worse than you think it is."

"It can't be worse than I think it is," snapped Nick.

"No? Well. Maybe. In the meantime, have you got anything you'd like to tell me privately?"

"A good deal. Come upstairs."

In the upstairs hall, the first person they met was a rapid-walking and somewhat upset Christabel. Christabel stopped short, turning her hands in a gesture of humorous consternation.

"That nice little child named Lisa," she began, "has been telling me—"

"Yes, ma'am," said H.M., ducking his head.

"What on earth can Larkin have been thinking about?"

"It was mostly my own idea, ma'am. It was strictly and personally my own idea."

"Dwight's told me *so* much about you. You'll stay with us, of course?"

"I'd be pleased to, ma'am, if somebody would lend me a toothbrush and a pair of pyjamas. I haven't got any luggage." H.M. stroked his chin. She returned his gaze smilingly. "I was just wondering whether I could see your husband."

"He's not conscious, you know."

"Yes. I know. I don't want to speak to him. I just want to see him. Y'see, I'm a medical man myself."

"But I thought you were a lawyer?"

"To sort of admit the guilty fact," said H.M., "I'm both. Can I see him, please?"

"Of course, if the Inspector doesn't mind. Dr. Clements is with him now."

H.M. turned to Nick. "This is important, son. It's maybe the most important thing in the whole ruddy affair."

"Go ahead, by all means. You might see me in the dining room later."

At his side, Betty shivered.

It might have been caused by the soggy skiing suit, or by something else. Waldemere was a hospitable house. A friendly house. A house full of pleasant people like Betty and Christabel and Eleanor and Commander Dawson. As Nick glanced round, he could see no element more alien than the harmless face of Mr. Naseby, looking at them from the doorway to the library. What, then, was the source of the evil which everybody knew to be here?

Betty felt it. Anticipating Christabel's third reference to her wet clothes, Betty turned round and hurried upstairs. She was followed by Christabel and H.M. Nick, in an enormous stillness, spoke across the echoing hall.

"Mr. Naseby, will you come here for a moment?"

Pause.

"You want to see me, young man? Very well. No objections."

Considering how well dressed the little man was, Nick thought, he might have got his hair cut: or at least what remained of the gray-black hair carefully plastered to his head. He crossed the hall firmly, without reluctance. But he seemed determined not to be helpful. He kept his mouth shut in a tight straight line, except when it became necessary to answer a question.

Nick stood aside so that his companion could precede him into the dining room, where Smeaton still waited.

"Would you have any objection to having your fingerprints taken, sir?" asked Nick.

Mr. Naseby gave no more than a glance at the crumpled El Greco by the sideboard, or the fallen silver and fruit. With surprising strength, using one hand, he drew out one of the heavy refectory chairs from under the table, placed it sideways, sat down on it, and drummed his fingers on the table. His mouth opened for one word.

"Why?"

"I can't compel you, of course—"

"I know that. I asked: Why?"

73

"You handled this fruit-knife last night, I believe?" said Nick, picking it up from the table.

"No."

"You didn't? Sure of that, sir?"

"To stab young Dwight? Are you crazy?"

"No, not to stab Mr. Stanhope. To pick it up from the floor after Eleanor Stanhope had started to peel an apple. There's a set of prints on it we haven't been able to account for. We think they must be yours."

He laughed at Mr. Naseby; and, after a pause, Mr. Naseby laughed back at him. He had rather bad teeth, Nick noticed. But a more law-abiding or less dangerous person than Buller Naseby, except perhaps in the business sense, it would be hard to imagine.

"Oh! If that's all?"

"That's all, sir."

"Then get on with your fingerprinting," ordered the other, sticking a thin, hard-veined wrist out of his sleeve. "I don't mind."

Nick made a gesture to Smeaton, who approached with inked roller, alcohol-dipped handkerchief, and card. While Smeaton worked, and Mr. Naseby watched curiously, Nick prodded him further.

"You haven't forgotten the incident of peeling the apple, have you?"

"Forgotten it? Not likely! The girl was drinking. Might have cut her thumb off. But would young Dwight say anything to her, no matter what she did? Oh, no."

"He's fond of her, naturally."

"Fond of her?" Mr. Naseby spat out the words. "He idolizes her. Ask anybody."

"Yes. But—"

"Of course, young Dwight's not a complete fool. No. If it's something important she wants to do, that's not so easy. But even then he never says, 'No - young - woman - you - can't - do - it - so - be - quiet - or - go - to - your - room,' as my father always said to my sisters, and as I'd say to my daughters if I had any. No: young Dwight must set out, quietly, to make her see for herself where she's wrong. Like that Dago courier in Buenos Aires."

"Yes, I see. The thing I actually wanted to ask you—"

"What that girl needs," declared Mr. Naseby, "is a husband."

"You think so?"

"I know so. None of these pipsqueaks. An older man. A man of the world. What'll happen to her if poor Stanhope . . . one of

74

the best friends I've got, mind you . . . what'll happen to her if he dies? He might. Even yet."

Smeaton had finished. Mr. Naseby, who in his Puritan earnestness had been poking his head first to one side and then the other in order to see past Smeaton and talk to Nick, received a handkerchief for wiping his hands.

Nick stuck to it. "About this apple-peeling business, sir. My question was this. *Did Mr. Stanhope himself touch the fruit-knife at any time?*"

"No."

"You're sure of that, now?"

"Dead sure, young man. Come to think of it, he didn't even touch the sideboard."

Smeaton, who was bending with a lens over card and powder-brushed knife at the far side of the table, now raised his head. His voice remained mild and colorless.

"In addition to being on the handle of the knife, Inspector," Smeaton reported, "Mr. Dwight Stanhope's prints were all over the top of the sideboard. Also on that silver fruit-bowl."

"Anywhere else?"

"The mantlepiece and the center table."

"What about the important exhibits? The electric torch? The El Greco?"

"Nothing on them except the smudges of gloves. There's other prints on some of the furniture, but all old ones."

Mr. Naseby was fuming.

"I can't help what your satellite says, Inspector," he interrupted angrily. "Young Dwight didn't touch either the knife or the sideboard. Ask Christabel. Besides, don't you remember it yourself? Weren't you here?"

"No."

"No, that's right! I remember now. You and Betty'd been upstairs. You walked in just as Eleanor and young Dwight and I came back from the dining room. Eleanor was carrying a tray of glasses."

True, Nick remembered.

He closed his eyes. He tried to recall every detail of that scene. Christabel by the fireplace. Vince James at the backgammon-table. Eleanor balancing the tray. Dwight Stanhope idling behind, his hands in his pockets. Naseby: no, Naseby's position remained a blank.

That whole trivial incident seemed to carry a muted significance, a meaning which just eluded him, a dim knocking against doors in the subconscious mind. Nothing had happened afterwards, at any rate. They had talked, in a desultory way, until half-past twelve; and then they had all gone to bed.

Nick opened his eyes again.

He had prowled in a circle round the table, oblivious of Mr. Naseby. He now found himself standing in front of El Greco's *The Pool*.

That picture had an elusive meaning too. Set against an arid landscape, Mexico or South America, a pool about the size of Kensington Round Pond was surrounded by a group of figures apparently preparing to dive into it. With consummate skill, the water was made to reflect their faces—and the expression printed on every face was greed. A figure suggesting a Christian friar stood in the background, pleading; while, behind a bush, something with a head-dress lurked and laughed.

It inspired distaste, but its power could not be denied.

"Admiring it?" asked Mr Naseby.

"Eh? No. I don't like it. Do you?"

"I don't understand art myself," said Mr. Naseby, with complacence. "Got no time for it. Though I daresay there's more meaning to that than to most of 'em, whatever it is."

He gave a brief, tight-lipped smile.

At the other side of the table, Smeaton looked up.

"This third set of prints on the knife-handle," Smeaton reported stolidly, "*is* Mr. Naseby's, Inspector. Just as we thought. So that's all right. He's on the handle with Mr. Stanhope and Miss Eleanor Stanhope, but nowhere else."

"Glad to hear it," chuckled Mr. Naseby. "Glad to show my innocence. Not that it was ever in question. Anything else I can do for you, young fellow?"

Nick walked back to the chair, where Mr. Naseby sat foursquare to the world.

"Yes," Nick replied. "You can tell me the real meaning of the term, 'the gilded man.' "

12

In the billiard room across the way, a game of table-tennis was in progress between Commander Dawson and Vincent James, while Eleanor Stanhope sat on the sidelines and watched.

The green-painted wooden board, with net, had been fitted across the top of the billiard table. Bright lights shone down on the table from under a hood with sloping sides. Beyond the windows—a long wall of close-set windows, made of colored glass blazoned with armorial bearings—you could see snow falling against dusk. Eleanor occupied a leather couch which ran on a sort of dais under these windows. Clear-curling yellow firelight showed the racks of cues.

"Nineteen. Twenty," counted Vincent James.

As he said twenty, his vicious swipe cracked the ball in a white streak over the net, to nick the edge of the table, fly off at an angle impossible to return, and subside in a series of small rattles as it bounced into a corner.

"Game," he announced. "Care for another, old man?"

"No, thanks," replied the Commander slowly. "That one hardly seemed to have begun."

"Now, Pinkey!" warned Eleanor. "You're not to lose your temper. Mind!"

By this time Commander Dawson's face as well as his hair did justice to his nickname. He made an interesting study in the rosewood-paneled room. Again he spoke slowly.

"It's these footling games," he complained. "If I get snarled up at anything important, it doesn't seem to matter. But a golf ball, or a ping-pong ball, or even one of those shake-the-box puzzles where you roll one little pellet in and all the others roll out, can arouse in me all the less presentable instincts of Attila the Hun."

"What's that, old man?"

"Nothing. Never mind."

"Table-tennis," Vince said sharply, "isn't a footling game. It's very good training for real tennis. Fred Perry—"

"He was standing too close to the table," interposed Eleanor. "Why didn't you tell him, Vince?"

"It's not my business to tell him, old girl. My business is to win. If he's fool enough to do that—" Vince's smile robbed the words of offense—"it's his lookout."

Commander Dawson contemplated him with real curiosity.

"Tell me. Is there anything you can't play?"

Vince laughed. He was pleased.

"Oh, I shouldn't like to say that. Got to keep your hand in at most things, of course."

"Lacrosse? Pelote? Baseball? Spit-in-the-ocean?"

"I never heard of Spit-in-the-ocean, old man."

"No, that's all right," said the Commander gloomily. "It's a card-game."

Vince picked up another table-tennis ball and began to bounce it on the table.

"I don't claim a very broad range, you know, Dawson. For instance, I don't know anything about boats—"

"Ships," groaned the Commander. "Great Christopher, *ships!*"

"Ships, then. Though I can't see why you navy blokes are so touchy about a ship being called a boat. After all, it is a boat or you couldn't sail on it."

"In it."

"On it or in it! All the same. As I say, I know very little about ships. Or paintings either, for that matter."

There was a silence, punctuated by the pock-pock noise as Vince bounced the little celluloid ball. Commander Dawson put down his racket on the table.

"Just exactly what did you mean by that?"

"Why, what I said," returned Vince, giving him a puzzled look. "You're the art-expert, or so Eleanor tells me. Each man to his trade, that's all. God knows you're welcome to yours."

Eleanor had been sitting with one leg tucked up under the other. A half smile showed white teeth against the tawny skin. Evidently she sensed tension in the air. She sprang up from the leather seat, jumped down off the dais, and ran to Commander Dawson.

"Pinkey, it *is* nice to see your ugly face again," she declared, throwing her arms round his neck. "But you mustn't let little things upset you. And you're all warm. Here."

Plucking the handkerchief out of his sleeve, she swabbed at his face with it. Now this is a process, however well meant, which never makes a man feel at his best. Added to the Commander's powerful diffidence whenever Eleanor approached him, it made him draw himself up as rigidly as though he stood before a firing-squad. Mr. James's amusement was no help. Suddenly Commander Dawson pushed Eleanor to one side: but gently, like one handling delicate glass.

"Have you got a trade?" he inquired.

"Well, old boy, I thought of studying medicine. Like W. G. Grace, you know. But I never could get past the first year, or remember anything except the funny bits."

"Funny bits," said Eleanor, "is right."

"When a lubberly seaman," said the Commander, "happens to take an interest in anything beyond navigation or gunnery, that's what's supposed to be funny. And when he takes an interest in pictures or—" He paused. "Good Lord!" he added, struck by a memory. "I forgot. Present."

"Present?" repeated Eleanor.

"I've got a present for you. It was a Christmas present, to be exact. But there wasn't any way of delivering it, so I thought I'd bring it myself. Er—I don't suppose you'd care to see the damn thing, would you?"

"Pinkey! How nice of you! I'd love to! Where is it?"

The Commander searched his mind.

"It's out in my bag, in the back of the sleigh."

"And where is the sleigh?"

"By the conservatory. I think. Hold hard. I'll get it."

"No, dear," corrected Eleanor, disengaging her arm from round his neck, "not that way. You surely must know the house better than that by this time. The room next to here is the library. The one in front of that is dear old Flavia's Oriental seraglio, after Brighton Pavilion. From there you can go through the conservatory, and out."

"Right. Thanks. Back in a moment."

When he had gone, Vincent James laughed long and loud; and the dark blood rose in Eleanor's cheeks. Eleanor, in fact, looked dangerous.

"Dear, dear!" she said. "Does anything strike you as being so especially humorous?"

"No. Sorry. He's not a bad chap, of his kind. Care for a game of billiards?"

"Thank you, no."

"Come on, old girl. Don't sulk! Have a game of billiards." Vince unscrewed the miniature posts of the table-tennis net, and folded it up. He slid the big board off the billiard table, and with a sudden heave lifted the table into the air.

Eleanor studied him.

"Of course," she said, "the idea of thoughtfulness of any kind might seem odd to you. I suppose you think thoughtfulness isn't consistent with manliness. Definitely, yes. It's all . . . is anything hurting you?"

"Only memory, dear girl," replied Vince, propping the board against the wall. "Only memory."

He turned round, walked towards her with easy assurance, and put out his hand. Eleanor backed away, but he caught up with her. He put his arms round her, bent her head back, and kissed her for about twenty seconds.

Eleanor disengaged herself. Though they stood in shadow, away from the table lamps, the yellow firelight rose up and shone in Eleanor's eyes.

"So Pinkey Dawson has come back," she said.

"Well, tigress?"

"And you can't bear anybody else to have anything," said Eleanor, "even when you don't want it yourself."

79

"Come on, little one. No fancy speeches. That was a parting kiss, with my blessing. Here, let's have another one."

After a pause, he added:

"Would What's-his-name Dawson do that to you?"

"Damn you. Let go."

"Now a final one. Just for luck."

This time Eleanor put her arms round his neck. She had to stand on tip-toe. The yellow fire crackled, shaking out sparks; beyond sham-emblazoned windows the snow fell with silent insistence; Eleanor uttered a little sob; the rosewood room was full of furtive shadows; and their position had not changed when Betty Stanhope opened the billiard-room door.

Betty turned quickly to go out. But Vince, with both eyes open, had seen her. He straightened up, dropping his hands. For the first time in months he looked as though he had done the wrong thing, and knew it. He walked across and made great play of selecting a billiard cue from one rack.

"I'm sorry," began Betty, who had changed her skiing suit for a dark frock. "I didn't think . . ."

"Why be sorry?" said Eleanor. "There's no harm done, is there? Got a cigarette, Vince?"

"You know I don't smoke, old girl."

"No, of course not. Bad for the wind, isn't it? Reduces the something-or-other. Got a cigarette, Bet?"

Eleanor, though languid, was breathless and a little hysterical. She still wore the slacks and the yellow jumper, which outlined the shape of her breasts. At her gesture, Betty picked up a cigarette box from a side table and held it out.

Vince looked at Betty. "I hope you didn't see anything personal in that," he said—and was surprised when both girls laughed.

"No, of course not," Eleanor assured him. "After all, Bet knows better than that. She was canoodling with the explorer last night, in one of the most romantic places in the house, so she ought to know better."

"What explorer?"

"Your friend. Mr. Wood."

"Go on!" said Vince, lowering the billiard cue.

"I tell you, it's true!"

Betty did not offer to explain. Picking up a table lighter, she snapped on its flame and held it out for the other's cigarette. These two, Betty and Eleanor, were genuinely fond of each other. Each (perhaps) had qualities that the other one lacked. But the situation at Masque House had become too emotionally complicated for everyday behavior. It became still more

80

difficult, a moment later, when Commander Dawson returned by way of the library.

"Here it is," he announced.

He was not the least surprised of them when Eleanor abruptly went to him and took his arm with a fervor she had never shown before.

"Pinkey Dawson, I could kill you!"

"Whang away with the knife, then," said the Commander cheerfully. "But why?"

"Just for being yourself!"

"Yes. I can understand that. Or, rather, I don't understand worth a damn; but it seems to please you, so that's all right. Aren't you going to open it?"

It was a ring, of heavy white gold set with a design of emeralds like a tightly tied knot. Eleanor unearthed it from a satin-lined box wound in tissue paper and plastered with Christmas stickers.

"Pinkey! It's beautiful!"

"You like it? You honestly like it? The knot's accurate," he was careful to explain. "First they did a thing like a granny. I made 'em reset it."

"But, dear—a ring! It's almost like an engagement ring."

"Is it?"

"Of course it is."

"Then have it as one," the Commander said loudly.

There was a silence. Moving with noiseless tread, Vince James set out the billiard balls on the table. His attention was absorbed in them.

"Pinkey, is this a proposal? In front of all these people?"

"They give me courage," said the Commander. "He either fears his fate too much, or his deserts are small, who—whatever the rest of it is. *Yes!*"

He roared this out.

"Any other bidders?" asked Eleanor.

"Eleanor!" said Betty sharply, and took a step forward.

Vince, utterly absorbed, bent over the green felt. His cue, sighted along the crook of a forward-thrust left hand, slid back and forth once or twice before it drove. The soft *click-click— click* as he effortlessly scored made the only sound there. Eleanor's expression was curious; a watcher might have thought that she was going to cry.

"It's not as though you could call it sudden," the Commander pointed out.

"Roy Dawson," cried Eleanor, "I'm not going to be swept off

my feet by *you*, of all people!" Her eyes blinked. "And at a time like this—"

"I forgot," Commander Dawson said quietly. There was a long pause. "Your father. Murder."

The word lay on them like a dead weight.

Vince circled round the table, eyeing it. "Excuse me," he said, politely elbowing the Commander out of his way. He bent over it, and the cue waggled again.

"It's not as bad as that!" put in Betty, with an effort at nervous tact. "He's going to get well. Mother even thinks we can have the entertainment tomorrow, with the conjuror and the cartoonist. She says the rector and Miss Clutterbuck have been ringing her up all day, and they'd never forgive us if we disappointed them."

Click-click—click.

"It was a lousy trick." The Commander touched Eleanor's arm. "Forget what I said. That's to say: don't forget it, but put it in cold storage until the old man recovers."

"Oh, you idiot!"

"As for the ring, stick it on another finger or wear it inside your shirt or something. I only got it as a Christmas present anyway."

"Look, dear . . ."

"I'll get you another one, with big diamonds in it, if you consider mine of the thirtieth ultimo., received, and report favorably upon same. Yes," he added in deep reflection, his gesture indicating something about the size of an alarm clock, "with big diamonds in it."

Click-click—click.

"Roy Dawson, are you going to listen to me?"

"In the meantime," said the Commander, "we've got to find out what happened to your father."

Vince glanced up and smiled slightly.

"Are you a detective, too, old boy?"

"I'm detective enough to see that the whole situation is phony."

"How?"

"If Mr. Stanhope had tried to steal his own Velasquez, that might have been all right. If he had tried to steal the Murillo, or the Goya, or any of the pictures upstairs, that still would have been all right. It might have been a rag of some kind. But since he had a try at the El Greco—well, I say he meant something by it."

Again there was a silence.

82

Three puzzled persons stared back at the Commander's long-nosed, long-jawed face. Eleanor, ring in one hand and cigarette in the other, looked helpless.

"Go on," said Betty.

"Well, see here! Is it a coincidence that that picture, *The Pool*, depicts the very scene of a business venture Mr. Stanhope's been asked to undertake?"

Vince put down the billiard cue.

"You may be making sense to yourself, old boy, but damme if you're telling us anything."

"I will try," retorted the Commander, rubbing his forehead, "to explain the not-very-baffling enigma in words of very few syllables. Let me first ask you a question. Did you ever hear of El Dorado?"

"Of course," said Eleanor.

"What was El Dorado?"

Eleanor frowned. "It was the City of Gold, mythical, that those old-time Spaniards were always trying to find and never did."

"What does 'El Dorado' mean?"

" 'City of Gold,' of course."

"Nonsense," said the Commander. "It means 'The Gilded Man.' And it's very far from being mythical. Read Prescott."

"The gilded man," repeated Betty softly. Her blue eyes were wide open. She put her hands to her forehead.

" 'One proper exploration of the pool,' " she said, quoting words she had heard before, " 'and all our troubles are over.' "

"So you know about it?" asked Commander Dawson.

"No, no! Go on!"

"The pool in question is Guatavita, the golden lake. I've seen it. It's in the Andes, within motor-drive of Bogotá.

"The Chibcha Indians poured their gold into it twice a year. I mean poured their gold literally. They did it in worship of the sun, taking the form of a deity called the Gilded Man, who was supposed to live in the lake. When Pizarro invaded Peru in the sixteenth century—the New Order, as usual—all the ruckus started."

Commander Dawson paused. He was obviously fascinated, though he would not admit it.

"Yes," insisted Vince, "but what's old Domenico got to do with it?"

"Look at the painting in the dining room!"

"Well?"

"It's what's called satire. Those are the treasure-seekers.

Look at their faces. They want to get to the bottom of that pool in spite of anything. And the Church pleads, and the Inca deity laughs, because they can't. They were trying to dredge or drain that lake in El Greco's time. They tried again at the beginning of the nineteenth century. They were trying, with modern machinery, as late as 1900. They've fished out very many thousand pounds' worth, of course. But the bulk of it is still there."

"Are you joking?" cried Betty.

Commander Dawson flushed.

"Don't take my word for it. Ask Mr. Naseby. He's got all the figures worked out."

"Buller Naseby?"

"Yes. He's been trying to interest your father in it. Your father just laughs at him."

"Now would you think," murmured Betty, wrinkling up her forehead, "that nice, dry, coupon-cutting man could have such a—well, such a romantic idea?"

"Oh, I don't know," said Eleanor. "I don't know. Anyway, Pinkey Dawson, you're being positively eloquent."

This in itself was enough to tie up the Commander's tongue. Becoming conscious of Eleanor, conscious of the ring which she had placed on the edge of the table, he hesitated. But he could not seem to help adding a last word.

"You see what I mean?"

"About what, dear?"

"About your old man! If a genuine burglar had gone for that El Greco, that would be understandable and wouldn't have meant anything. But, since it was your father who picked it out, I still say he had a reason."

"That is," Eleanor said, "if he knew what the picture represented himself. There's nothing to tell you in the composition."

"He didn't know, until I told him," admitted the Commander. "But he's known for months. What about the rest of you? Curse it all, haven't you got any curiosity about old masters?"

"Don't look at Vince, dear," said Eleanor gently. "He's not concerned with old masters; only with young mistresses. As for me, no. There was a monk in it. I thought it was religious. So I wasn't interested."

"But the point is . . ." urged Betty.

"Yes." Eleanor grinned a wicked grin which seemed to animate her whole body. "Buller Naseby."

"This buried treasure sounds to me like a lot of rot," observed Vince, after careful consideration.

"Vince! How terribly romantic you are today! Let's," suggested Eleanor, "let's get dear Buller and toss him in a blanket. He's been so close-mouthed that it hurts. What does *he* say?"

13

"That's what I've got to say," Mr. Naseby spoke coldly. "It's all I've got to say."

Looking Nick straight in the eye, he rose from his chair by the dining-room table, consulted his watch, and replaced it in his waistcoat pocket.

"Twenty-five minutes of bulldozing. No; twenty-six. Anything else, young man?"

"Recovering the gold of the Chibcha Indians." Nick studied the El Greco. "You don't tell me, sir?"

"I do tell you. Perfectly straight business proposition. No particular secret about it."

"No. Still, did either you or Mr. Stanhope happen to mention the proposition to any of the people here?"

"Mention business to women? Not likely!" The man's exasperation so tautened him that he seemed to be rising on the tips of his toes. His small black eyes, under wrinkled lids, never left Nick's face. "Nor young Dwight either, if I know him. Why should we?"

"Yes. At the same time, you've acknowledged——"

"Under bulldozing."

"Under questioning, that you knew this picture depicts Lake What'sitsname, where the stuff is buried." Nick touched it. "Then why not say so at once? Why have the information dragged out of you?"

Mr. Naseby corrected him, with grim amusement.

"I know what young Dwight *said* it represented, that's all. Have I any proof of that? No. Does it look as though it represented Lake Guatavita? No!" Suddenly he chuckled. "Give away information, unless I have to? Not likely!"

"That's all, then. Good day, sir."

Mr. Naseby took three steps towards the door before he swung round.

"Young man, you're cleverer than I thought. You got it out
85

of me. But you won't get anything more. Don't try. Good day."

And, in going out, he almost collided with Sir Henry Merrivale coming in.

"H'mf," sniffed H.M., surveying the daubs of gray powder which besprinkled the room. "I see you've had a fingerprint man here. Where is he?"

"Gone. I sent him away when I pitched into our friend Naseby."

"Naseby? Would that be the cocky little feller who just went out?"

"Yes. Have you found anything?"

H.M. looked awed. "Have I found anything? Have I *found* anything? Oh, my eye." He stumped over to sit in the chair vacated by Naseby. With great difficulty he fitted his ample proportions into it, wheezed, peered over the tops of his spectacles, and took from his pocket a case full of black, oily-looking cigars.

"Tell me, son," he added. "Have you got Dwight Stanhope's burgling clothes? Where are they?"

"They're locked in the wardrobe of his dressing room upstairs. I had a run through them early this morning: especially the contents of his pockets. Then I ticketed 'em and put 'em into a suit-box. Would you like to see them?"

"I should, son. No end."

Nick rang the bell for Larkin, who answered it with suspicious celerity. Larkin colored up (if this can be believed) when he saw H.M., but neither of them spoke. Nick gave the butler the key to the wardrobe and his instructions. While he did so, H.M. scratched a match to flame on his thumb-nail, and lit one of the oily cigars. His eyes roved round the room, coming to rest at last on the sideboard.

"Now, then!" Nick turned back. He indicated the El Greco. "Do you know what that is?"

"Uh-huh," said H.M.

"Yes, it's the famous El Greco. But can you tell me what it represents?"

"Uh-huh," said H.M., taking the cigar out of his mouth. "A conception, allegorical, of Lake Guatavita in the Andes."

Nick stared at him.

"Deduction, sir? Or information received?"

"Neither, exactly. Eavesdroppin'." H.M. looked uncomfortable. "Your friend Betty Stanhope came downstairs. I followed, to ask a question. She started for the billiard room. So did I. She opened the door, unfoldin' a tableau of considerable interest. She didn't quite close the door."

"And you listened?"

"Sure." H.M. gave a sketch of it, omitting certain details. "Very interestin'. Yes. So."

"Look here, sir, is this Lake Guatavita on the level?"

"Oh, son! It's the most famous lake in South America."

"I mean, is there really any gold in it?"

"There is. In addition to centuries of offerings to the Gilded Man, a local caique, or big shot, chucked in two tons of loose stuff to save it from one of Pizarro's captains named Quesada. They burnt the caique alive for that little bit of nose-thumbing; but they didn't get the dibs. It began the quest for El Dorado. Even Sir Walter Raleigh had a shot at it."

H.M. pointed one finger.

The painting had its own leer. Steel-gray water, peer of reflected faces where mendicant and court lady knelt side by side, backs crouched on those who prepared to dive: it remained violent with life, even crumpled before a sideboard in an English home. Where Dwight Stanhope had been lying, a few drops of blood had now dried to rust-color against the black carpet.

H.M. stared fixedly at those spots, before returning the cigar to his mouth.

"But if the stuff is there, sir, why can't anybody get it?"

"Item," said H.M., "the lake's over two hundred feet deep—"

"Difficult, yes."

"Item, there's been centuries of mud, rocks, and sand washed down into it since then. *Item,* even when you get the lake drained, and it's been drained, there's still a cup-shaped mud-hole leadin' to points unknown. Still, with modern engineerin' methods, you might do it. It'd cost money. But you might do it."

"Then Naseby's idea's not so wild after all?"

H.M. considered.

"Not so wild, no. But rummy. Exceedingly rummy from a steady-going City man."

"Would you, for instance, put money into it?"

"Well . . . now. I might. But that's because I like a sportin' go. Even before you started hauling your pumps up eleven thousand feet of steep mountain, you'd still have to get a concession from the Colombian Government. And that might take Rockerfeller's back teeth."

"You see," Nick explained, "Naseby wants Mr. Stanhope to go half shares in the venture."

"Does he, now?"

"Yes. I happened to overhear a conversation myself, last night in the little theater upstairs."

"Ho, ho," said H.M., an expression of wooden glee stealing across his face. "Was that when you were canoodling with Betty Stanhope?"

"Where did you get hold of that?"

"Never you mind where I got hold of it," said H.M. darkly. "Burn me, I dunno what the police force is coming to," he added, shaking his head. "I can remember a time, not so long ago either, when your boss Masters nearly ran me down and killed me because he was tryin' to assault a lady in the front seat of a car."

"I wasn't canoodling with her! I thought about it, I admit. But she'd only have walloped me anyway."

"You think so?" inquired H.M., with infinite pity like St. Francis. "You think so? Did you ever see her when you weren't looking at her?"

"No, sir. Very seldom."

"And no smart cracks, either," said H.M. sternly. "What's more, son, you be careful. She'll be a rich woman one of these days."

"That doesn't worry me. I don't think I ever mentioned it, but—never mind!" Nick flung away the personal issue. "I'm on duty, damn it! It doesn't matter what I like or don't like. And all these people . . ."

"Yes. All these people." nodded H.M. He puffed slowly and deeply at the cigar, until his head was surrounded by a poisonous cloud of smoke. "Lemme see. The bloke in the naval uniform, I gather, is a certain Commander Dawson: Mrs. Stanhope was telling me about him. The curly-haired athlete is your friend Vincent James. And the little dark devil who bounces is Eleanor Stanhope, apple of the old man's eye."

"Yes. Speaking of apples, that's the fruit-knife. There on the table, beside you."

H.M. picked it up, while Nick retailed the evidence of the fingerprints. He was still talking when Larkin returned with the cardboard suit-box.

Nick put the box on the table. It contained thin kid gloves, a black mask, a muffler, a tweed cap and coat, corduroy trousers, a wool shirt, an undervest and underpants, socks, and tennis shoes. In his pockets—arranged in a neat line by Nick —Stanhope had been carrying a handkerchief labeled D.S., two valueless letters addressed to him at Waldemere, a glass-cutter, a clasp-knife, and a small roll of surgical adhesive tape. A wrist-watch completed the list.

"Excuse me, sir," interposed Larkin, hesitating at the door.

Both Nick and H.M. looked up, the latter with an expression of slowly deepening depression.

"Yes?"

"I was to inform you that tea will be served in the lounge in ten minutes."

"Right. Where's the lounge?"

"The Oriental room, sir. And one other thing, if I may ask." Again Larkin hesitated. "Would it be possible, sir, to clear this room today? So that meals can be served here as usual?"

Past cigar-smoke H.M. spoke with fierce, growling intensity.

"No, son, it wouldn't."

"Sir?"

"With the Inspector's permission, you can say it'll be a long, long time before anybody ought to use this room. Maybe till pigs fly and billiard balls grow whiskers. Oh, Lord love a duck!"

"Very good, sir," said Larkin, and went out.

One by one H.M. examined the articles in the victim's pockets.

"The glass-cutter," explained Nick, "we can account for. The clasp-knife is undoubtedly what he used to cut the picture out of the frame. It certainly wasn't used to stab him; there's no blood on it and, anyway, the blade is much too thick."

"Yes," grunted H.M. flatly. "Yes. Quite."

"Part of that adhesive tape was used on the window over there, put on in short strips, to keep the glass from falling." Nick made an illustrative gesture. "But I'd like to call your attention, sir, to another queer fact about it."

"So?"

"Pick up the roll of adhesive tape, and look at the loose end of it," suggested Nick. "Wait! Here's a lens I borrowed from the library early this morning."

He produced the lens and handed it over. H.M., the cigar stuck at an angle in the side of his mouth, held up the tiny roll and peered through the lens at the edge of the loose end.

"Blood!" he said.

Nick nodded.

"Yes, sir. Blood. It's easy enough to reconstruct what happened, but as to *why* it was done . . .

"Like this," Nick went on. "The murderer stabbed Mr. Stanhope. Then he stamped on him as he lay on the floor. Next, while Mr. Stanhope was unconscious, the murderer took that roll of adhesive tape from his body, and cut off a piece of tape with the blood-stained fruit-knife. That's what he did, right enough."

89

"H'mf, yes. I sort of think so myself, son."

"But what did the murderer want with a piece of adhesive tape? Why did he do it?"

" 'Why' again. Uh-huh."

H.M. handed back the tape and lens. He removed the cigar from his mouth and put it carefully on the edge of the table, where it sent up a straight line of oily gray smoke. Putting his hands to his temples, H.M. ruffled the fingers over his big bald head.

Nick gathered up the articles.

"These clothes, according to Mr. Stanhope's valet—"

"Lemme think!" H.M. suddenly roared. "For the love of Esau, lemme *think!*"

For some time he remained sunk in obscure meditation, tapping his fingers on his head.

Then he got up. His eyes, blank, followed the pattern of gray-daubed fingerprint powder across the room. From the wall containing sideboard and door to the main hall, he faced about to the wall directly opposite.

He lumbered across to it and inspected Velasquez's *Charles IV* at the left of the fireplace. He inspected Murillo's *Calvary* over the fireplace. It was only when he came to *The Young Witch,* at the left, that he recoiled.

"Cor!" said H.M., with awe. "Who's been buyin' up the furnishings of a brothel?"

"That's art."

"Not to me it's not," said H.M., putting his bald head on one side and studying the picture. "I got a simple straightforward mind."

(Like the devil you have. What are you up to?)

"It belonged to Flavia Venner," said Nick.

"Oh, ah. The wench who owned this house. Sort of ghostly atmosphere of her floatin' about."

Again he turned round. His expression was still a blank. Putting his fists on his hips, he once more blinked across at the sideboard over his spectacles.

"I say, son. Did that sideboard have a runner on it?"

"A what?"

"A runner. You know. Sort of narrow cloth thing that they put on sideboards and tables to keep ornaments from scratching the surface."

"No, there wasn't a runner. I'm certain of that. Why do you ask?"

H.M. pointed a big flipper.

"Well, don't it strike you that all the loose silverware on the floor is lyin' a good deal in one place? A few round pieces have rolled, yes, and pretty wide. But look at the heavy stuff. It's almost as though, while Stanhope and the murderer were fightin', somebody had grabbed the end of a runner and yanked the whole mess sideways. Or else . . . is any of it scratched, by the way?"

"Yes, several pieces."

H.M. peered backwards over his shoulder at the fireplace. Then his gaze moved across in a diagonal line to the sideboard again. A sort of dismal astonishment showed in his face before the face smoothed itself out to impenetrable dullness.

"Y'know," he breathed, "that's torn it."

"What's torn it?"

"You'd never guess," said H.M.

Nick's mania of curiosity had now reached close to boiling-point. He was about to indicate this when they were interrupted by a light tap at the door.

"I thought I'd knock first," remarked Christabel Stanhope, "in case you were measuring footprints or something. May I come in?"

She spoke in a high, thin, clear voice. From the moment he heard that voice, and saw Christabel's hands, Nick sensed trouble ahead. She carried her own emotional atmosphere, which was usually one of smiling placidness. It had changed now.

H.M. remained deliberately obtuse.

"Tea, ma'am?"

"No. Not tea. There's . . ."

"Would you care to sit down, ma'am?"

"Beside all those horrible things on the table? No, thank you."

At a gesture from H.M., Nick cleaned away the debris, including fruit-knife and electric torch. H.M. picked up his cigar, and Christabel consented to take his chair. She had a crumpled handkerchief clutched in one hand, and in the other an ivory compact which was also a cigarette case. She added:

"Will you close the doors to the drawing room, please?" Nick obediently rolled them together. "Will you also promise that nothing I say here will go any further?"

Danger! Look out!

Nick shook his head.

"I'm afraid I can't promise that, Mrs. Stanhope."

"Why not?" asked Christabel, rapping the compact on the arm of the chair.

"An official code called the Judge's Rules . . ."

"Sorry. You misunderstand." She tried to smile at him. "Let me put it like this. Last night you told me that you, an official detective, had been sent here, first—" she lifted one finger —"because Dwight has considerable political influence; and, second—" she lifted another finger—"to head him off and prevent scandal if he should attempt a fake burglary for the insurance."

"Yes, Mrs. Stanhope?"

"Dwight has done well. I don't deny it. But I can't help feeling, somehow, that he hasn't got *quite* as much influence as that. In fact, you yourself admitted that there was still another reason why you had been sent here."

Nick inclined his head.

He wondered if she had guessed that reason.

As he nodded, so did Christabel. Her mouth was slightly open; the nostrils of the short nose a little distended. Her right hand clamped the handkerchief, her left hand the compact, to the arms of the chair. The skirt of her tea gown, a sea-green, reached to the floor. She turned her head towards H.M.

"Sir Henry, you're well acquainted with Dwight?"

"Yes, ma'am," returned H.M., leaning one elbow on the sideboard and watching her. "I think I can say that."

"But you weren't acquainted with the details of his various business affairs?"

"Oh, ma'am! That's a bit of a tall order. No. I don't expect anybody was, except himself."

"Would it surprise you, then, if anybody called him a thief?"

H.M. blinked at her. "It'd more than surprise me. I wouldn't believe it. As I was tellin' this young feller today—"

"You still don't follow me. I don't mean a sharper or a swindler. I mean a literal thief."

Her broad mouth tightened.

"Would it surprise you if someone said that the bulk of Dwight's income comes not from any business dealings, but from burglary? From a few carefully selected raids on art treasures, months or years apart: any one of which would keep us all in funds for a year?"

14

"One moment!" Christabel added sharply.

But neither of her companions spoke.

"You understand, I don't believe it. It's absurd and ridiculous and humiliating. But you might as well know—" suddenly she put up her hand, and dabbed the handkerchief between her eyes—"it's what they're saying in the servants' hall.

"It will be all over the district tomorrow, and all over the county the next day. Never mind whether we're criminals: the point is, we shall be laughing-stocks. Even if it isn't true . . ."

H.M. took the cigar out of his mouth.

"Well, Lord love a duck!" he exploded, with such violence that Christabel lowered the handkerchief to look at him. "So *that's* what's been worrying you, is it?"

Christabel tilted her chin in the air. "Really—" she began coldly.

"Oi, now!" persisted H.M., waggling the cigar at her. "It is what's been worrying you, isn't it? I thought there was somethin'."

"And if it were?"

"In fact, you more than half believe it, don't you?"

Christabel did not reply.

H.M. expelled his breath.

"Mrs. Stanhope, no wonder Flavia Venner is your favorite heroine. You got an imagination like Ouida and Marie Corelli rolled into one. Ma'am, I can lay my hand on my heart—" here he did so— "and swear Dwight Stanhope is no more a burglar than I am. If you don't believe me, ask Inspector Wood."

Nick nodded.

"He's right, Mrs. Stanhope," Nick answered truthfully. "Mr. Stanhope isn't your super-burglar, whatever else he may be. We never thought he was."

H.M. looked apologetic.

"But that's not the interesting point, ma'am. The interesting point is: How did you come to get such a pleasantly loopy notion?"

Christabel made a gesture.

"I tell you, they're openly saying it in the servants' hall!"

"Oh, that?" H.M. was unimpressed. "Yes. I knew that."

"You knew it?"

"Sure. I spent some time there, you understand." He turned to Nick. "The theory there, son, is one you mayn't have heard. Dwight Stanhope is close-mouthed. Ergo, he's mysterious. The newspapers this last year have chronicled one or two juicy country-house burglaries—"

"Yes, they have." Christabel spoke through her teeth. "I mentioned it to Inspector Wood last night."

H.M. glanced at her sharply, but continued:

"Dwight Stanhope dresses up as a burglar, and is found

under somewhat rummy circumstances. First conclusion: he was just goin' out to crack another crib, probably Buller Naseby's house. Second conclusion: somebody in this house spots him, mistakes him for an intruder here, stabs him, and then takes a peek under the mask and finds with horror that it's the old man. So the person in question hares away before the alarm, and won't own up even yet."

Christabel did not speak.

Her shiny-looking eyelids were lowered. She seemed to be studying the tips of her dark-green shoes. But Nick could sense about her an intense watchfulness.

"Of course," H.M. growled, "that theory won't explain the cut window-pane or the almost-pinched El Greco. But you can't have everything. Ma'am, that's not good enough."

"I don't want everything," said Christabel. "I want—well!"

"That's to say, ma'am," explained H.M., "that fun and games below-stairs oughtn't to bother you as much as that. But you are worried. No end. Why is it? Why this obsession about a burglar, and your husband in particular?"

"I'd like to know the answer to that too," said Nick. "After all, Mrs. Stanhope thought *I* was a burglar last night."

Christabel eyed him with reproach.

"My dear man, that was only a dream. And I told it to you in confidence."

"Dream?" exploded H.M. "What dream?"

"Oh, I dreamed all sorts of ghastly things. It was just some talk of the night before: mixed up, as I told Mr. Wood, with what I'd read in the papers. Perhaps I wasn't quite frank with you about all of it. But when I came out and found you in the hall, and then Dwight downstairs stabbed—" She paused. She spoke quietly. "You're not trying to trap me? You honestly don't think Dwight was even mixed up in any crooked dealings of any kind? You swear that?"

"I swear it, Mrs. Stanhope," replied Nick.

Christabel sat back. It was an odd transformation: as though her face, which had grown faintly withered, got back its bloom again.

"I don't know how many burglaries you have in your books for the past year," she said. "But I can recall two country-house ones. One was at . . ."

"Cataract House, Crowborough, June the eighth," supplied Nick.

"And the other at . . ."

"Pensbury Old Hall, Yate, September the twenty-seventh."

94

"Thank you, Inspector. My husband was a guest at the house on both occasions; and I wasn't there.

"Please don't run away with the idea that *I* ran away with the idea. But it did seem, since then, that references to pictures or rare manuscripts or precious stones were always cropping up. Dwight wasn't himself, either. On top of that, in walked a a stranger, a presumed friend of Dwight—" she looked at Nick—"who was obviously not what he pretended to be."

"Thanks," grunted Nick.

"You were seen coming out of Dwight's room. When I spoke about it to a friend, I covered it up by suggesting you might have been ransacking it. Actually, you were talking to Dwight. Weren't you?"

"Yes, Mrs. Stanhope."

"You see, I thought you might be his accomplice. Then, when you did seem to be a bona-fide police officer, that was even more horrible. I thought you must be after him for attempted insurance-fake. Finally, all this talk among the servants—

"You men dismiss that, don't you? But it *is* important, whatever you say. The sillier the rumor, the sooner it spreads. I can stand most things, but I can't stand being laughed at. We've had enough subtle digs from our friends about this house. I love this house. So they can all go, if you will excuse me, straight to hell. But no more, please. No more."

She inclined her head at them, a twinkle in her eye and the curl of a smile round her lips. It was a consciously graceful movement of the head, like that of an actress. Overhead lights caught the waves of her silver-streaked hair; it brought out, by contrast, the youthfulness of the face.

"Oi!" said Sir Henry Merrivale, almost gently.

His powerful voice was subdued.

"I've been standing here, all quiet and peaceful," he pursued, "waitin' for some enlightenment. What's all this about burglaries at Crowborough and Yate? What burglaries at Crowborough and Yate? Masters didn't say anything about 'em. *You* haven't said anything about 'em, son. What is all this?"

"But don't you read the police news?" demanded Nick.

H.M. shook his head with decision.

"Not about burglaries, no. Burglaries aren't interesting, except topsy-turvy ones like this. The professional criminal is the dullest dog on earth. I wouldn't walk across the street to see Charlie Peace steal the Lord Mayor's trousers."

Christabel made a face.

"That was another thing," she smiled. "Comparing Dwight to Peace of Peckham Rye. Oh, yes they did! Lisa told me so. Awful double life. Oo! It may seem funny to you, but it wasn't to me. Tell me, Sir Henry. Was Charles Peace really an artist in crime, a poet and a violin virtuoso?"

H.M. peered at her over his spectacles.

"No, ma'am, he wasn't. His verses would make a school-song writer writhe and his famous violin was a cigar-box fiddle with one string. He was just as oafish as the rest of his tribe."

"You could hardly say that—" Nick spoke with care— "about *this* fellow."

Something in his tone caused a slight pause. The sway of crimson curtains, still drawn close before one open window, caught the corner of Nick's eye.

"Oh?" said H.M. "You mean the Crowborough and Yate man? You think the two jobs were done by the same feller?"

"Yes. We think so."

"And what's so special about him?"

(Christabel's eyes, Nick noted, were brilliant.)

"He knows pictures, he knows jewels," Nick answered, "as any Bond Street dealer would give his soul to know 'em. Do you want instances? At Pensbury Old Hall there was a gallery full of expert fakes, mostly bought as originals, and one smallish, genuine Leonardo. Our man lifted the Leonardo alone.

"At Cataract House, in June, he passed over a sackful of showy stuff, good but not outstanding, in order to take just one string of matched emeralds nearly as valuable as the other lot put together. Am I talking too much shop?"

"No," smiled Christabel. "I rather think you're giving yourself away."

"Am I, Mrs. Stanhope?"

"Come now! That final reason why you were sent here! The reason you wouldn't tell me! Can you deny it was to be on guard, here in a house full of valuable if not tasteful things, in case the Crowborough-Yate gentleman paid us a visit?"

Nick lifted his shoulders.

"I don't deny it. I told you Chief Inspector Masters didn't neglect any bets. But—"

"Yes? *Do* go on."

"It doesn't work. First, your husband did this little fake here. Second, in case you think I'm calling him the criminal after all, I can tell you that the technique of this job was utterly different from the Crowborough-Yate bloke. You can always spot 'em by their technique.

"Third, the fake burglary hasn't anything to do with the at-

96

tempted murder. It wasn't the burglar who stabbed; it was the burglar who *got* stabbed. That brings in the other element we've got to account for. Hatred."

Again the word seemed to hang with cold ugliness. Again it produced its effect.

"Sir Henry!" said Christabel.

"Ma'am?"

"I hardly like to admit it," Christabel spoke lightly, "but this man scares me. He really does. When we go back to the eternal refrain of hate, hate, hate . . ."

H.M. had seemed sunk in obscure musing. Now he roused himself. His cigar had gone out. He put it down on the sideboard.

"I'm afraid we've got to go back to that refrain, ma'am. It's at the bottom of everything. Trace it back, and I've got a ghosty kind of idea we've got all our answer. This business, d'ye see, is no plain Charlie Peace affair: shoot-the-constable-and-over-the-wall. It's clever and it's ugly and it's deformed. Of course, the solution of the problem itself may be simple. . . ."

"Simple?" shouted Nick. "You call this tangle simple?"

H.M. was somber.

"Yes. Looky here, son. Don't be misled by trappings." He swept his hand round. "I told you before, it's Flavia Venner's influence. This ruddy house is haunted by romantic possibilities that aren't true."

"That," observed Christabel, regarding him sideways, "is rather shrewd of you."

"But the key that unlocks the door is different. I've got a sort of idea, y'see, that the solution can be given in just two words, by answerin' a certain question."

"If we could only talk to Dwight himself!" Christabel complained. "When will that be possible, do you think?"

H.M. hunched up his shoulders. "I dunno, ma'am. Tomorrow maybe. He's under an opiate now. As Dr. Clements may 'a' told you, these internal-bleeding cases are the devil. If you could do a nice post-mortem, you could diagnose like billy-o; but you can't very well do that if you want the poor bloke to live."

"And by tomorrow," Christabel said wryly, "it will be all over the place that Dwight is Charles Peace or Deacon Brodie or the Man with the Twisted Lip."

"Are you goin' to stop this nonsensical worrying," demanded H.M., "or aren't you?"

"Sorry," shrugged Christabel. "I can't help it. I don't fuss; but I worry. Do you remember the Man with the Twisted Lip, Sir Henry? He also had a fine house in Kent, yet he actually made

97

his living as a professional beggar on a street-corner. I wonder what *his* wife thought, when she heard? If Miss Clutterbuck or the rector hear about Dwight, I imagine they'll forbid the children to come to this wicked place for the conjuring entertainment."

H.M. was caught by a new, gripping interest.

"Hold on!" he said. "Conjuring. Has this got any reference to the feller I was mistaken for?"

"I'm terribly sorry about that."

"Oh, ah? But who is this Great Kafoozalum, anyway?"

"Ram Das Singh. He's all the rage in London. He's a real Hindu."

"Is he, now?" sneered H.M., with immense and lofty contempt. "*I* never heard of him."

"He's given Command performances, Dwight says. His props arrived this morning, but I haven't had any telegram to say when he'd arrive himself. You'll probably enjoy meeting him. Eloise, that's my maid, says you gave a very fair little parlor-show yourself."

H.M. spoke with terrifying slowness.

"A very fair little . . ." He paused. "I s'pose you think." he said, "that this Ram Das Ruddy Singh is a better conjuror than *I* am?"

Christabel smiled. "Well, Sir Henry! You may be a very distinguished amateur, of course—"

"Amateur!" said H.M., suddenly turning purple in the face, and raising both fists. "Amateur. hey?"

Nick felt that it was time to interfere.

"It's all right, sir. I don't think for a minute this Ram Das Singh could manage the Indian rope-trick. You'd probably beat him hands down."

"I'm sorry." said Christabel, puzzled to have made a slip-up in tact. "Have I said anything I shouldn't?"

"No, Mrs. Stanhope. And, anyway, it's hardly the point. Even if Mr. Stanhope does recover, we've still got a pretty ugly situation here. Sir Henry tells us, and seems to believe, that he can explain the whole problem in two words . . ."

H.M. stared at him.

"Ho? You think I'm goin' to tell you," he said, "after the insults you've just been showerin' on me?"

"Damn it all, sir, I didn't insult you! Every time somebody says or does anything you don't like, you turn around and swear it was me. This is getting to be a bit too much. I've tried to keep my mind on business . . ."

98

"I wonder," observed Christabel, in a pleasant but meaning tone.

"Pardon?"

"You certainly frightened Betty." Still Christabel spoke with detachment. "She had the same doubts as I had about Dwight's double life. You didn't improve her state of mind by what you said to her, whatever it was, up in the little theater last night."

"But, Mrs. Stanhope—"

"The poor child came into my room this morning to talk. A thing she hasn't done in years. At first she thought you were Dwight's accomplice, just as I did. When Mr. James passed her on the stairs and said, 'Your father dressed up as a burglar and somebody stabbed him,' she thought *you* had done it. Afterwards she was conscience-stricken, and said she wanted to be especially nice to you today."

So that was it!

Nick had much to think about. And, when he thought of Betty now, it hurt him to draw the breath through his lungs.

"I regret, Mrs. Stanhope," he said, "that I seem to be the villain of the piece all the way round."

Christabel recognized the fencing approach.

"The villian of the piece? My dear Mr. Wood! I'm afraid Betty has cast you in quite another rôle." She shrugged and touched the handkerchief to her lips. "That is no business of mine. Dwight and I don't interfere with our children."

"Unfortunately, the question is who—you can say interfered, if you like—interfered with Mr. Stanhope?"

"I loathe your pertinacity," said Christabel.

"And yet, d'ye know," interposed H.M. unexpectedly, "the lad's quite right."

"Thank you," said Christabel.

"Horseradish!" said H.M., not gallantly. "I'm the old man. I'm impolite. But then everybody kicks me in the pants and gets away with it, so a little refreshin' candor on my part is permitted by the best authorities.

"There's a murderer here, ma'am. Murder was done in intention if not in fact. It may be tried again. I'll bet you ducats to an old shoe that it would have been tried again, if this feller hadn't arranged to have somebody sitting by your husband's bedside every minute of the night or day."

"You think that?"

H.M. snorted.

"Think it! Cor! I smacking well know it! Look at the evidence. Do a little sittin' and thinkin' for a change. One thing that's as plain as beans is this: Dwight Stanhope mustn't wake

99

up. There's a special, strong, agonized reason why he mustn't. Further. Somebody, smallish or of rather light weight, has stamped on him and kicked him in the head—"

"Did you say small," interrupted Christabel, "or of rather light weight?"

It was fully ten seconds before H.M. responded. The corners of his mouth were turned down.

"That's the medical evidence," he said. "Doc Clements deduces it from the comparative lightness of the bruises round the head: where, *pace* anybody, he was kicked, not stamped on. You can tell that from the size of the bruises. It's pretty suggestive, don't you think?"

Christabel lowered her eyes. When she raised her head again, she had left the defensive and become human again.

"Sir Henry," she said, "pity a lone lorn person whistling in a graveyard. That's what I've been doing. I hate thinking about unpleasant things. As a rule, I won't think about them. I've been trying to avoid this. And I can't avoid it. It's no good. The fact is, somebody did that to Dwight."

She threw her handkerchief on the table. She put down the now moist compact beside it.

"But who did it?" she added: not loudly, but with a clearness of enunciation which rang in the bright room on a note of desperation or anguish. "Who did it? *Who did it?*"

15

Far away, the church clock over the fields struck the hour of one in the morning.

Masque House was silent. Most lights were out. Most guests were abed. But no person, except Dwight Stanhope and some of the servants, had gone to sleep. Eyes were still open, brains moved, emotions stirred, at the turn of the dark hours while the snow still fell.

In his bedroom up on the first floor, the owner of the house lay like a dead man except for his slow breathing. It was the most austere room at Waldemere. A muffled lamp in a corner faintly illumined Stanhope's strong nose and jaw. In a wing chair near the bed, Hamley sat and drowsed. Sometimes he would start up, raise his head suddenly, and glance towards the bed. But nothing moved here, not even a shadow.

"Blighter!" Hamley said.

Downstairs, in the library, Sir Henry Merrivale sat bolt upright, like a stuffed owl, in front of a low fire.

They had given him a pair of Dwight Stanhope's pyjamas. Hamley also unearthed Dwight's dressing gown from the wardrobe in the dressing room, after swearing it had not been there in the morning. Both pyjamas and dressing gown were much too long, but the pyjamas just managed to meet round H.M.'s capacious middle, and the dressing gown would not meet at all.

Behind him, three lofty walls of books rose into dimness. The flicker of firelight, from under a carved overmantel as big as an arch, moved on carved bookcases broken only by the line of the windows. It flickered on heavy chairs and a table with a white-feather quill pen stuck into the inkstand. Marble busts, after the Victorian fashion, looked out from the tops of the bookcases.

Whether H.M. should have been at home in company with Socrates, Thomas Carlyle, Pallas Athene, and other persons whose meeting in real life must have precipitated a truly memorable row, still he did not look at home.

Clearly there was something on his mind.

Poker-players at the Diogenes Club do not get far in attempting to read his face. Still, since he was alone, his expression might have been called one of malevolence and irony. He occupied a leather chair. His slippered feet were planted wide apart. His elbows were bent, his hands on his knees. A stout monkish figure trailing blue wool, with the stuffed-owl aspect apparent in his face, he peered over his spectacles at the fire.

"Phooey!" said H.M.

Eleanor Stanhope was a little tight.

Not much, but a little. As she heard the clock strike one, she was just pouring out a nightcap from a flask kept as an emergency measure in the drawer of her dressing table.

Her rooms comprised a suite on the first floor, front, across the gallery from Christabel's. Eleanor fetched a tooth glass out of the bathroom, and poured whisky into it. Her look indicated that she would have just this one: no more. Then she would turn in, and be able to sleep.

Eleanor's yellow silk pyjamas were the color of her room. The glass of the etchings on the walls reflected back images of the bedside lamp. (In fact, Eleanor's "Have-you-seen-my-etchings?" was a reverse-twist of the old one.) She had scrubbed her face, revealing faint lines under the eyes.

All evening she had been trying to get Commander Dawson drunk.

As a result, she was half-whistled herself.

On the bedside table lay a ring set with emeralds, beside the house telephone. She stretched out her hand, either towards the ring or towards the telephone. Then she drew back. She lifted the glass and gulped down its contents. As she reached to turn out the lamp, her expression was the fiercely martyred one of a woman who knows she can never sleep.

The bedclothes had been turned down. Eleanor swayed as her knee struck the side of the bed. She crawled in, fell back, and was instantly asleep.

"Darling!" was the last thing she said.

Vincent James half-dozed in darkness.

Yet a dim suggestion of light from the snow entered through the windows: both of which, as a matter of health, were wide open. They looked out over the flower garden, or what in remote ages might have been the flower garden, from the first floor at the back. A breeze stirred in the Arctic room. Snow ticked softly at the windows. A flake blew across and touched his forehead.

He stirred and muttered. He was not asleep; he was at that stage where the mind seizes on a trifle and turns it into something of monstrous importance. A personal worry, a question left unanswered during the day, some point noticed but not quite understood. Some perplexity of this kind appeared to be gnawing at him now, seeking the answer to what he had observed.

"Doctor?" muttered Vincent James.

As the clock struck one, Betty Stanhope turned on her light again.

She must face the fact that she couldn't sleep.

Any observer, too, would have seen more: an observer would have seen that she was afraid.

Betty's room was on the second floor, above her mother's. No other member of the household ordinarily slept on this floor, though tonight Commander Dawson had been put into a guest room across the gallery. This floor contained the picture gallery, a ballroom at the back, a nursery more forlorn than any place in the house, and guest bedrooms. On the story above this, the attic, slept the servants. Above the attic, sixty feet up, towered the cupola which contained the miniature theater: and above that swirled, like a dance of the imagination, the limitless acres of night-sky.

Was that a noise, then?

Ordinarily Betty never minded the isolation of this floor. She liked it. She could read as late as she liked without having somebody put a head in and talk about her eyes or health. Tonight, or this morning, the hollow rooms shut her in; light merely peopled the darkness outside; the twitch of a curtain twitched nerves as well.

Betty sat back against the pillows, one hand on the chain of the reading-lamp fixed to the head of the bed, the other clenched on the eiderdown.

"Nick!" cried Betty Stanhope.

Naval men, notoriously, have heads like Gibraltar.

Commander Dawson, sober as a temperance hotel on Sunday, and fully dressed except for his jacket and collar, was pacing up and down the Regency guest room across the gallery.

The Commander had very steady nerves for any job of work. But he did not seem easy now. He lit a cigarette, put it down on the chest-of-drawers, and, after an interval of deep pondering, lit another. They had been made by a famous Egyptian firm, and were carried duty free. The Royal Navy is not unduly troubled by customs inspection at ports.

From time to time the Commander would glance at a picture of Eleanor Stanhope, in a leather frame, which stood exactly in the middle—Roy Dawson was a tidy soul—on the top of the chest-of-drawers. Before he retired he would put this picture back in his suitcase, in case the maid who brought him his tea next morning should think him a sentimental goop.

From time to time, also, the writhing of his face would have alarmed any person who was not a medical man. He seemed to be cursing himself.

Why the hell, he seemed to be saying, did you have to go and blurt out a proposal of marriage in front of everybody? Well, what of it? They didn't laugh, did they? No; but they probably split their sides in private. You're a fathead: you know that, don't you? Yes! Would you do the same thing again? Yes!

Presently his pace slowed down. His expression became not so much self-accusatory as thoughtful. Wrinkles, like comma-marks, deepened round his mouth. He nodded to himself.

"Diamonds!" whispered Commander Dawson.

The room below Betty's had belonged to Flavia Venner.

Now, as in other days, Flavia's portrait by Sir Edward Burne-Jones hung above the fireplace.

Now, as in other days, after a current fashion, the walls had

103

been cushioned in upholstered satin with rows of buttons to give shape to the upholstery, like a sybarite's padded-cell. Here Flavia could look into one mirror, and meet herself coming out of three or four others.

At the moment, this could not be so much seen as traced out, line by line or surface by surface. The curtains were not quite drawn. One window stood open half-way. At some distance across the hills, street lamps of a built-up area made a hazy blue twinkle behind the falling snow. Though the room itself was dark, the ghost of light entered when Christabel Stanhope, sitting at the window with a fur coat round her shoulders, drew back the curtain part way.

Christabel drew the coat closer.

Her chair creaked. Dinner that night had been an uncomfortable affair, served in the wrong room and therefore giving all the guests a sense of intrusion. So Christabel would have answered, if she had been asked her thoughts. Her long, slender fingers let the curtain drop. She yawned, with pleasant tiredness; perhaps a warning reflection that things could have been much worse, after all. She reached her arms above her head, stretching.

"Clever?" said Christabel.

It was at a quarter past two in the morning when Nick Wood hit on the clue he had been looking for.

By this time, the others were all asleep. But a dogged young man, sitting up in bed with a notebook and pencil, kept his light burning.

He shut up his mind to all personal considerations. What worried him most was that there seemed no place to make a beginning. So far, his work had been among the smaller fry of professional criminals: the routine work which individualists like H.M. hated, and which he himself conceded to be dull enough. But there, at least, you had a starting point. From the technique of a job, you could argue that there were half a dozen professionals who might have done it. Find out where persons A to F were at the time, and you were half-way home.

Here, however, the evidence was less like a series of trails than like a circle of burrs. You turned it in your hands without being able to decide what was start, middle or finish.

Nick smoked cigarette after cigarette without inspiration. In desperation, after still another reading of his notebook, he tried the Chestertonian principle of looking in the wrong direction: of making his mind a deliberate blank and seeing if anything welled up from the so-called subconscious.

Infernal nonsense, of course. Still . . .

His thoughts, released, instantly flew towards Betty Stanhope. He dragged them back again. A picture of Masque House rose in his brain, high and square and smooth. He thought of Christabel in the dining room, which led back to Betty. He thought of snow, which led back to Betty.

"Steady!" he said, and pressed his hands to his forehead.

If he were to concentrate on H.M.'s actions that day, he might catch the great man's mental coat-tails and follow H.M.'s path towards a possible solution. The first picture to rise in his mind was that of H.M. getting a snowball in the schnozzle, which was not very helpful. Then an impression of H.M. performing sleight-of-hand in the servants' hall, while an insistent voice called for the Indian rope-trick. No good. The Indian rope-trick suggested rope, and rope suggested . . .

Very slowly Nick sat upright in bed.

"Wow!" he said aloud.

The house was very still. M. Marcel Proust himself would have had difficulty in tracing the memory lines Nick tried to assemble. A piece of information offered by Buller Naseby flowed in among them, along with another picture of a few seconds past, and formed a moving pattern.

Listening to the busy ticking of his watch, he glanced sideways. His eye fell on the house telephone beside it on the bedside table. It was a quarter past two. To wake anybody up at this hour would be an outstandingly dirty trick. Besides, there might be no more in his idea than a false brain spark like the snap of a defective cigarette lighter.

But he was damned if he could go to sleep until he knew. He took up the phone, and jabbed at one of the white enamel buttons.

"Hello!" he called. "Hello!"

And he continued to jab until a voice, heavy and throaty with sleep, spoke back to him.

"Hello? Is that you, Larkin? Inspector Wood here."

"Yes, sir?" If the butler's soul breathed a curse along the wire, Nick did not hear it.

"I'm sorry to disturb you at this hour; but it's something very important to the investigation."

"Yes, sir?" Larkin, coughing the frog out of his throat, sounded almost eager.

"You remember the information I asked you to get for me last night? I mean, Thursday night? About ways of getting into the house? You told me about it this morning."

"Yes, sir?"

"You said you examined the downstairs windows. Did you by any chance examine the upstairs windows too?"

Larkin sounded surprised. "I did, Inspector. I understood that was required."

"You did?"

"Yes, sir."

"Then listen carefully. Did you see anything hanging out of any of the windows?"

"Sir?"

Nick gripped the telephone. "I don't want to put any ideas into your head. You may have to testify to it. I mean just exactly that. Did you see anything hanging out of any of the windows?"

"No, sir."

"But did you have a look at all the windows?"

"Yes, sir. Miss Eleanor and Miss Betty were already downstairs, if you remember, and I had no hesitation about entering their rooms."

"Let's get this very clear," Nick insisted. "This afternoon, in the basement, I happened to hear somebody—I think it was the chauffeur—mention that in the bedrooms there's a coil of rope hooked to the wall, for getting out in case of fire." He peered sideways. "In fact, there's one here behind the curtains."

"Yes, sir. The Southerby Patent."

"There wasn't a rope hanging out of any window, then?"

"Definitely not, sir. I could go further and say I was certain none of them had been disturbed."

There was a pause.

"That's all, then. Many apologies again for getting you up like this."

"Not at all." The telephone suddenly chuckled, becoming human. "If it's about detective work, sir, just you get me up at any hour you like. I've often thought I had a bent in that direction myself. Just as, if you'll pardon my mentioning it, I know a bit about medicine, too."

"Yes. You saved the situation when my foot slipped about Mr. Stanhope being dead. Thanks. Good night."

"Good night, sir."

Nick replaced the telephone.

He found and lighted another cigarette; he discovered, with detached astonishment, that his hands were shaking and that unconsciously he was holding his breath.

Once able to make a start, Nick had felt, he might at least be in a position to go forward—slowly. This was not going slowly. This was flying, as with the rush of skis down a slope. Yet the

106

thing remained inescapable. If *a* were so, it followed that *b* must be so. And *c,* therefore . . .

He wondered if H.M. had followed the same course. He doubted it. H.M. followed a short, direct track of his own. Yet both, it might be, were converging from different directions on the same point.

Nick set his mind on this. Drawing in a deep inhalation of smoke, he blew it out and watched it drawn, like a moth, into the light of the lamp, where it wove and fanned and curled up above like altar-smoke. He had some distance to go yet. But, once past the first ingenious bit of misdirection, it was possible to see the clearest of good reasons in what had seemed unreason. Dwight Stanhope had been no fool or practical joker. In the thing he did, he had never acted more sanely in his life.

"Played!" said Nicholas Wood.

16

Saturday morning, New Year's Eve, dawned over a countryside so deep in snow as to resemble a dead world. The sun, a dim orange-glowing disk, illumined little more. At Waldemere it struck through the windows of the library, where Christabel Stanhope and Sir Henry Merrivale were sitting after breakfast.

And there was now in progress a telephone conversation of even more direful results than that of the night before.

"This is Miss Clutterbuck speaking," announced the telephone on the library table.

"Yes, Miss Clutterbuck," replied Christabel. "Larkin told me."

When speaking to Miss Clutterbuck, it was necessary to hold the receiver at least six inches away from the ear. She had one of those voices which pierce carbon. You cannot help imagining that, by some witch's spell, the woman herself has dwindled and is imprisoned inside the phone, where she sits talking away like a machine-gun and making the whole phone shake.

"An invigorating morning, is it not?" shouted Miss Clutterbuck. "I trust Mr. Stanhope is better?"

"Much better, thank you."

"I am gratified to hear it. I am de-*lighted* to hear it. The dear rector is delighted to hear it. And by the way, I must tell you—" here Miss Clutterbuck gave a bark of laughter which made Christabel jump—"that the most extraordinary and comical rumors have been reaching me."

"Yes, Miss Clutterbuck?"

"I understood from you (please do forgive me for mentioning this) that Mr. Stanhope met with an accident as the result of a Christmas game?"

"Yes, Miss Clutterbuck."

"How extraordinary stupid people are! Still, one does feel that it is one's duty to protect the little children from malign influences, *wherever* they are found."

"Yes, Miss Clutterbuck."

"Now about this afternoon's entertainment," proceeded Miss Clutterbuck briskly. "I shall be grateful if you will have not less than fifty folding chairs in the auditorium. I must ask you, furthermore, to have—"

"Just a moment, please, Miss Clutterbuck!"

"Yes?"

"I'm afraid I've got some rather bad news. The cartoonist can't come."

"Well, really!" said the telephone, freezing up.

"And that's not all. We've just had a telegram phoned in. It was handed in at Manchester yesterday. Yes, Manchester. It says . . . Wait—I'll read it to you."

Christabel picked up the desk pad.

"'AM DEEPLY APOLOGIZING SNOWSTORM IS IN-TERFERING WITH LOCOMOTION OF UNDER-SIGNED.' Stop. 'CANNOT REACH YOUR HOUSE TO-MORROW.' Stop. 'NOT HOME YESTERDAY YET.' Signed, 'RAM DAS SINGH, THE GREAT KAFOOZA-LUM.'"

There was a long silence.

"Did you hear me, Miss Clutterbuck?"

"Yes, Mrs. Stanhope. I have often said that a little *care* in managing these matters, a little *foresight*, which people will *not* take the trouble to exercise, would do much towards avoiding the quite unnecessary difficulties in which they find themselves."

"Wait, please! It's all right, that part of it."

"Indeed?"

"Yes. A friend of ours, a distinguished amateur—"

H.M. was sitting on a sofa, a toothpick in his mouth and an expression of dignity on his face.

"—has kindly consented to take over the other man's props and appear himself as The Great Kafoozalum."

"They were *promised* Ram Das Singh, Mrs. Stanhope."

"I'm very sorry; but under the circumstances . . . ."

"And who is this amateur of yours, may one ask?"

108

"His name is Merrivale. Sir Henry Merrivale."

There was an even longer pause.

"My dear Mrs. Stanhope," said Miss Clutterbuck, a faintly different note creeping into her voice, "did you say Merrivale?"

"Yes."

"Not *the* Merrivale? Of Cranleigh Court, near Great Yewborough?"

"I—I don't know."

"You don't know?"

Christabel put her hand over the mouthpiece of the phone. "Do you live near Great Yewborough?"

"Uh-huh," said H.M., taking the toothpick out of his mouth. "Why?"

"Yes, Miss Clutterbuck."

"My dear Mrs. Stanhope, I'm sure we shall be only too delighted to bring the children along. They do so enjoy conjuring. Of course, you would not mind if I were to change my mind from my decision the other day, and bring a friend or two of mine?"

"Please do."

"Sir John and Lady Minsterstroke. Major Babbage. Mr. and Mrs. Talbot. Such nice people. Miss Durne. Mr. and Mrs.—"

"Yes, of course."

(Have we got enough food for all those people?)

"I believe the entertainment starts at four? Good. We shall be in ample time. Until then, dear Mrs. Stanhope!"

Christabel put back the receiver, and raised her eyes to heaven.

H.M. fixed a malignant eye on the telephone.

"Is that gal anything like what she sounds like?" he asked.

"She's just what she sounds like."

"Is she now?" mused H.M., very thoughtfully. He fixed his eye dreamily on a corner of the ceiling.

A babe in arms could have discerned that he was plotting devilment. But he did not continue. Nick Wood, charging into the room with a theory full grown, stopped short.

"Good morning, Mr. Wood," said Christabel. "You look as though you hadn't slept very well."

"Good morning, Mrs. Stanhope. I'm all right. I only—"

"Had your breakfast?"

"Yes, thanks. Sir, I wonder if I could have a word with you?"

H.M. gave him a sharp look. "About what, son?"

"About the solution."

"That?" said H.M., with austerity. "I got no time to bother

109

with that. I got to concentrate. I got to rehearse. I got to practice."

"The Great Kafoozalum is storm-stayed in Manchester." Christabel smiled. "Our friend is going to take his place on the platform." A frown deepened on her smooth forehead. "It's awfully kind of you, but, really! is it right to open the poor man's apparatus and use it without even consulting him?"

"H'mf. Well. It's not strictly ethical, no."

"Besides, you haven't even seen it! You don't even know what his tricks are!"

"Have no fear, madam," declared H.M., extending a hand, palm outward. "If there's any flummery that's ever been invented, I know the priniciple of it. You just trust the old man. Burn me, I'll give 'em such a show as they'll never forget."

Again the telephone rang.

Snow lay in drifts two feet deep against the library windows. The brown curtains were drawn back against dusky, orange-shot daylight. From the tops of the bookshelves, marble busts looked across at each other with ineffable detachment. A big blaze crackled in the chimney, meeting daylight with shadows, as Christabel again took up the phone.

"It's for you," she said to Nick. "Toll call from London. Will you take it here, or from another room?"

Though he did not like to take it here, Christabel's eyes challenged him. He accepted the phone.

"See here, my lad," spoke the sinister voice of Chief Inspector Humphrey Masters, "what have you been doing to the old man?"

"What old man?"

"Sir Henry. He says you hit him in the mush, whatever that is, with a snowball."

Again Nick counted slowly to ten. He wondered if he would ever hear the end of the infernal incident.

"I didn't do anything of the kind. I only knocked his hat off. It was Miss Stanhope who hit him in the mush."

"Well, you be careful! How're things? Have you made any progress?"

"Look, sir, I can't talk now . . ."

"Oh, ah?"

"But you can take it from me that avenues are being explored, and one of them leads straight to what we want."

Masters whistled.

"Does it, now? That's smart work, Nick. *If* it's what we want. What does Sir Henry think?"

Nick turned his eyes towards the leather sofa. To his surprise,

110

H.M. had gone; H.M. was not anywhere in the room. Noiseless exit for a man of his bulk could not have been easy. But it enabled Nick to speak his mind.

"He won't say anything. All he does is talk about a conjuring show he's going to stage this afternoon. He's got hold of a lot of apparatus belonging to a magician called the Great Kafoozalum."

There was a brief silence.

"Goddelmighty!" whispered Masters.

Now it may be remembered from other cases, notably the Plague Court affair,* that magic was Chief Inspector Masters's hobby: a hobby gained from deep experience with card sharps and bogus mediums. Nick was therefore prepared to listen with respect to anything he said on this subject. And Masters was saying plenty.

"But isn't it all right, sir? He tells me he knows the principle of every trick in the box."

"Oh, ah! Yes! He knows the *principle*. He knows how. And he can handle small stuff. But he can't manage gimmicks. He's as clumsy as a bear in a zoo. Do you realize it takes weeks of practice just to get one little effect right? And he takes over the whole caboosh . . . Stop a bit, though!"

Nick could hear Masters breathing heavily along the line. Then the chief inspector spoke in a thoughtful tone.

"Tell me, Nick. Dead set on this show, is he?"

"Yes."

"Won't say a word about anything else? Glares you down if you as much as mention business?"

"Yes."

"Just so. That's what I thought. Then you let him alone, my lad." Masters spoke casually. "I've seen this happen before. He'll help catch a murderer for you, and maybe our jewel-lifting bloke as well."

"But how can he catch a murderer by sawing a woman in half or taking colored ribbon out of his mouth?"

Pip, pip, pip buzzed three clicks in Nick's ear. "Your three minutes are up," caroled the girl at the exchange.

"Ring you later," said Masters, and the line went dead.

Christabel, who had put on a pair of reading glasses with huge white rims and stems, sat by the table reading the morning paper with every appearance of absorbed interest. It must be a heroic delivery man, Nick reflected, who brought newspapers on a day like this.

* *The Plague Court Murders*, by Carter Dickson, William and Company, 1934.

111

"If you're looking for him," remarked Christabel without glancing up, "you'll probably find him in the little theater. He said he was going to get Betty and Eleanor for his assistants."

Nick had almost reached the door before she spoke again.

"Er—Mr. Wood!"

He swung round.

"I looked in on my husband before breakfast." Christabel took off her glasses. "He spent an easy night and his temperature is almost normal. He'll be able to talk today, won't he?"

"We think so, Mrs. Stanhope."

"And, Mr. Wood!" She was going to speak about Betty, he guessed; he could almost feel the atmosphere. But Christabel changed her mind. "Nothing," she said, and put on her glasses.

On his way up to the roof, Nick stopped in the gallery to look into Dwight Stanhope's room. Though the curtains had been pulled back before murky daylight, the muffled lamp still burned in its corner. Hamley, in correct black, nevertheless looked more haggard and hollow-eyed than the man on the bed.

He had a grievance which would not be denied. Selecting Nick as a kindred spirit, he poured it out.

"I tell you straight, I'm just about fed up," Hamley muttered. "If old Larkin *wanted* me to drop down and sleep in the hall, he couldn't go about it no better."

Both of them kept their voices studiously lowered.

"Been up all night?"

"Yes. But it's not that. It's doing it all the time. Jack Emory relieves me in ten minutes. But I've got to come back on again at three in the afternoon. Same yesterday. You remember, when you and Miss Betty came downstairs, the buzzer went for me sharp at three?"

Nick nodded. Hamley pressed his hands over his eyes.

"The poor old governor can't help it," he added, jerking his head towards the bed. "It's this blighter Larkin." He mimicked. " 'There's a show in the little theater at four, my lad; mind you don't nip up for a look at it.' Me! God's truth! As though I could nip upstairs to see Tommy Farr knock out Joe Louis!"

"Sh-h!"

The bed, of heavy dark wood, stood with its head against the right-hand wall. On the table beside it Nick noticed two medicine bottles standing in a saucer, a spoon, a cut-glass pitcher of water, and a bakelite cup. The austere dark-blue hues of the room seemed to throw their effect across Hamley as well. He mopped the sweat of exhaustion off his forehead.

112

"And I can tell you," he said, "it wasn't half creepy in here last night."

"Nothing happened?"

"No. I couldn't say it did. Only half the time I imagined somebody was looking at me from the door."

"Imagination, as you say."

Hamley was bitter. "Maybe it was and maybe it wasn't. What with things disappearing and turning up again, and the governor (as I told you before) buying clothes in secret that I never saw before, you can say it's all imagination he's laying there with a sticker-cut in his chest and three ribs caved in.

"God!" Hamley added suddenly, in turning to point. *"His eyes are open!"*

The words, commonplace in themselves, had an edge of superstitious terror flung out by lowered vitality. It was as though Hamley had spoken of a dead man.

Both he and Nick moved quietly across to the bed. Rolling away a blue-cushioned wing chair, Nick bent over. Stanhope's darkish gray hair was not much ruffled. His long body appeared bulky under the eiderdown, from the dressing of the ribs. The hands, with their short square-tipped fingers, were spread out. His face had the same mildness as in waking moments, a serenity only marred by the dark bruises along the side of the head. Even these, except the bruise below the ear, were mainly concealed by the hair and by the sinking of his head into the pillow.

His eyes, as Hamley said, were wide open. The eyes moved, without curiosity, as though studying the range of the ceiling.

"Mr. Stanhope," Nick whispered.

The man's gaze continued to rove, right and left. The fingers of one hand twitched, as though to move up and feel his chest.

"Mr. Stanhope! Can you hear me?"

"He can't hear you," Hamley muttered, plucking at Nick's sleeve. "Come away. Leave him alone! The doctor said to leave him alone."

"Mr. Stanhope!"

Dwight Stanhope looked him straight in the eyes.

Hamley uttered a stifled exclamation. Between eerie daylight and the glimmer of the brass fretwork lamp in the corner, the hurt man's countenance appeared pleasantly normal. Only the bruise below the ear showed as a brush of evil.

Over a straight chair near the bed still hung the dinner jacket he had taken off late on Thursday night, to put on other clothes. The studs remained in the shirt, the shoes and socks on the floor. Hamley had been told not to put them away, and they remained. Nick could see them with a new eye now. But he was not looking at them.

"Mr. Stanhope, my name is Wood. Do you recognize me?"

Stanhope's tongue crept out to moisten his lips. Delicate bones, thought Nick. Brittle bones, for all that well-knit appearance.

"Mr. Stanhope, you've been hurt. But you're better, much better. Can you speak now? Don't speak if you don't feel like it."

The eyes remained without life or curiosity; and yet, as though beyond Dwight Stanhope's own volition, a dull gleam crept into them.

"Will you walk into my parlor?" he said clearly.

That was all. The wounded man's face twitched. Something seemed to move inside his chest, like the bump of clockwork. His eyes closed.

Hamley's hoarse cry was shushed by Nick, who himself felt a rush of alarm. But he need not have feared. Stanhope's breathing was steady, his pulse reasonably normal. He was merely sleeping the light, worried sleep of a man who has returned to the world again.

17

In the theater upstairs, H.M. leaned one elbow on the miniature-bar counter, and pondered.

"I don't care what you say," Betty was insisting, "I won't wear tights, and that's all there is to it."

"Prude," grinned Eleanor. "Dear old Bet!"

"It isn't prudery. It really isn't! It's only that there's something silly about tights. I can't tell you why I think that; but they don't seem to be one thing or the other. Besides, we haven't got any."

"No," Eleanor admitted. "There's that."

"And in front of Miss Clutterbuck? You know we couldn't do it. She'd never forget it."

"Looky here," interposed H.M., coming out of his trance to regard them sternly. "If you don't want to wear 'em, don't wear 'em. Wear your best bib-and-tucker. Wear any blinkin' thing you please. Only for the love of Esau let me concentrate!"

Nick, finding his way up a last flight of stairs, discovered them here. Betty still remonstrated.

"In all seriousness," she said, "do you honestly think we can get away with this? Eleanor and I have absolutely no knowledge of conjuring."

"And I keep tellin' you," said H.M., "that you don't need to. Except the Vanishing Lady and the Levitation; and I can teach you that in ten minutes. All you'll have to do, mostly, is hand me things when I call for 'em." He scowled. "Burn me, though, I don't like that stage!"

He surveyed it. A high, carpeted dais in an arch, it was the core of the somber gray-and-gold theater. Sniffing, H.M. backed away to the panel of lights beside the door. He experimented, flicking switches on and off. Lights appeared, vanished, darted, and ran in waves. They glowed yellow under cornices. They appeared from the wings, and under the proscenium-arch. They broke out of the ceiling. They flashed behind glass prisms against gray-curtained walls.

Under these rippling contrasts, Eleanor's black skirt and scarlet blouse made her resemble a figure out of Peer Gynt. Betty, in white, was Faust's Marguérite. Commander Dawson, sitting in one of the embryo boxes with his feet irreverently on the rail, could only have been Commander Dawson.

H.M. made a grudging concession.

"Not bad, though," he said. "You tell me there's a trap-door in the floor of the stage?"

"There are two," Betty informed him. "Flavia went in for all sorts of mysterious effects. It's hard to see the trap-doors, even close at hand, because the design in the carpet hides them."

"Uh-huh. Where do they go?"

"To the floor below. The two dressing rooms are down there, next to the servants' quarters."

"Curtains?"

Eleanor ran across to the stage, leaped up on it, and disappeared round the arch. First a motion-picture screen, weighted at the bottom, shot downwards and hung wavering. There was some rather vile profanity from back-stage. The screen rolled up jerkily, and was replaced by two gray silk curtains which swept out from either wing and swirled together.

"There you are," called Eleanor, sticking her head out between the curtains. "If you want to blot out the mantelpiece at the back, you can do that, too; there's some more curtains."

H.M. was still manipulating lights. Their alternate flash and darkening had a bad effect on the eyes. Once they went out altogether, and Betty called a nervous protest. In the act of switching them all on again, H.M. caught sight of Nick.

"If you're chasin' me," H.M. said malevolently, "don't."

In fact, Nick noted in a dispirited way, his entrance was greeted by everybody except Betty as a dash of cold water.

"Oh, Inspector, be a sport!" Eleanor burst out. She jumped down from the stage, went to H.M., and hooked her arm in his. "No questions now, please!"

"I wasn't going to ask any questions. I only—"

"This is New Year's Eve. Can't you forget business just for once? Have a drink! Or do you drink?"

"Certainly I drink. I only—"

"Look here, the Inspector's quite right," observed Commander Dawson. He unhooked his feet from the rail of the box and got up. "We'll not get away from the unpleasantness of this business by play-acting. Ask your questions, old man. I know Eleanor will help you."

"No, I won't," Eleanor said peevishly. Her voice grew honeyed with coaxing. "Inspector, darling! *Please!* Try to be a nice man for once."

Nick drew a deep breath. Bile rose in his soul.

"Very well," he said. "I give up. To hell with the whole thing."

He took his notebook out of his pocket, and only instinctive caution prevented him from firing it across the room.

"As you say, this is New Year's Eve. If you think I don't want to enjoy myself just as much as you do—never mind. No more questions! None, whatever happens! If there's any way I can help with the show, I'm at your service."

Eleanor beamed at him.

"Darling!" she chortled. "That's more like you! Then you've heard? Homer here—" she pressed H.M.'s arm—"is going to be the Great Kafoozalum. We're going to get him up like a real Hindu, so the kids won't know the difference."

"Good. Anything I can do?"

Eleanor considered.

"Well, we're going to show Homer how the trap-doors work. But I expect you and Betty: you know what I mean?"

Eleanor did not say this as a joke or a sly thrust. She was quite serious. Whirling round again, she urged H.M. and Commander Dawson towards the stage. Her eager voice continued as though there had been no interruption.

"You heard what Betty said. There are two traps. One on the left and one on the right. The one on the left is straight. I mean, it's on a hinge; and you climb down through it on to a step-ladder or whatever you like.

"But the one on the right is great fun. It's like a lift. There's a crank and a windlass down below. You stand on it; and the whole square of the trap moves up and down. Homer, I warn you: this show of yours will have to be awfully good. Miss Clutterbuck is keen as mustard on magical secrets. She had an uncle in Edwardian days who was a personal friend of J. N. Maskelyne, and she hasn't forgotten it."

H.M. directed a curious backward glance at Nick as Eleanor bore him away, with Commander Dawson on the other arm. Nick could hear them stumbling down some narrow stairway beyond the proscenium arch.

Throughout this, Betty had not spoken a word. She was behind the bar counter, vigorously mopping its polished surface with a cloth.

There was a silence in the dim, circular theater after the others had gone. Nick went across to the bar and climbed up on one of the stools.

Still silence.

Putting down the cloth, Betty abruptly turned round to the rack of bottles. She twisted a tap, drew a glass of whisky, and pushed it across to him along with the soda syphon.

"I know exactly how you feel," she said, with her eyes still on the counter. "Drink that."

"At ten-thirty in the morning?"

"It won't hurt you. It'll do you good."

Nick slowly turned the stem of the glass round on the counter. He searched desperately for conversation. Betty went back to mopping again. There was, he noticed, again a full saucer of potato chips on the counter; and this reminded him.

"Will Mr. Naseby be here for the show today?" he asked.

"Yes, naturally. He always is. Why?"

"Nothing. Tell me, Miss . . . look here, I'm going to call you by your first name. Do you mind?"

"You sound like Roy Dawson," said Betty. "Of course not!"

"Well, then. Why *did* they call this Masque House?"

The hand holding the cloth stopped.

"Flavia Venner's theatricals," replied Betty, glancing up briefly, "were supposed to be very wicked. People didn't want it known that they came here. So Flavia said that everybody, figuratively, wore a mask; and while they were inside these walls you weren't supposed to know what their real faces were like."

From somewhere, vaguely under the stage, they could hear muffled conversation, a squeal from Eleanor, and a bump.

"Here's Larkin!" they dimly heard Eleanor cry. "Larkin, be a dear and work the windlass for us. It runs on counterweights; it's as easy as grinding a barrel-organ."

Nick continued to twist the stem of the glass.

117

"Masks!" he said. "Yes. That's it! We've been fooled by as ingenious and artistic a mask—"

"Figuratively?"

"Figuratively, yes. As ingenious and artistic a mask as I ever came across. Also, the only kind that would be convincing." His mind, still astonished, went back over it.

"Oh!" Betty cried involuntarily.

Nick craned round to follow the direction of her glance towards the stage. The gray silk curtains were now drawn back again, exposing a dim cavern. Nick started to laugh, but checked himself.

Like a demoniac illusion, or the effect of a guilty conscience in somebody's morality play, the head and shoulders of Sir Henry Merrivale were rising up through the floor of the stage. A square opening yawned about him. The trap moved soundlessly, on oiled cogs. His waist and legs soared into sight. The carpet closed with a soft bump, leaving him there.

H.M. destroyed the illusion with a loud sniff. Also, it was he who appeared to have the guilty conscience. After hesitating as though swearing at himself, he stepped off the trap, climbed down off the stage, and approached Nick.

"See here, son," he growled, after glancing round to make sure they were not overheard. "Do you think, have you got an idea stuck in your head—well, burn it all!—that the old man's not attending strictly to business?"

"You're a free agent, sir."

H.M. pointed a finger at him.

"Oi, now! None o' that! Don't you, of all people, start to act like a kid with a sore head. You think I'm just messing about, don't you?"

"Yes."

"Well . . . now. Maybe I am, a bit," H.M. admitted. "For years I've dreamed of gettin' an opportunity like this. You don't understand the philosophy of conjurors, son."

"No."

"No. The true-blue conjuror is a simple soul devoted to his art. He don't ask for money. He don't ask for laurels. All he asks for is an opportunity in front of an audience, any audience, that won't run screaming towards the nearest exit as soon as he starts to roll up his sleeves. That," said H.M., with unusual candor, "is what they're always doin' to me. Do you understand?"

"Yes, I think I do."

"But if you think," said H.M., significantly closing one eye, "that I'm exactly forgetting all about other things—"

118

Nick felt a great relief.

"I see. The chief inspector said you might be up to something."

"Oh? So Masters is buttin' in again, is he? He thinks *he's* a conjuror. What'd he say?"

"He suggested we might compare notes."

"H'mf! Well! I got no objection to that, son."

"Then tell me this. What's the main problem?"

H.M. pondered deeply. He rubbed a hand across his bald head, scratched the side of his jaw, stroked his chin, and shook his head.

"The main problem," he replied at length, "is the dress suit. I got an Indian turban, of course, from some fancy-dress stuff the little gal dug up. The trouble is, d'ye see, I haven't got a dress suit with the proper pockets for loads. I wouldn't have had a dress suit at all, if the housekeeper hadn't offered me one that belonged to her late husband. He got killed in a . . ."

"Sir Henry!" said Betty.

"Hey?"

Betty leaned across and touched him gently on the sleeve.

"I honestly think," she continued, nodding towards Nick, "that you're going to have Inspector Wood in a fit if you go on like that. He wasn't talking about the conjuring show. He was talking about the situation here."

"Then why in blazes couldn't he say so?" retorted H.M.

"I did say so."

"All right, all right! Keep your shirt on, son. One thing at a time."

H.M. became very quiet, his fists on his hips.

"Somethin' gave me an idea," he went on, "that you think you've spotted the answer to the whole business."

"Yes. I think I have."

"So! In that case, I'll ask you just one thing. There are lots of ways of approaching it, but this may be the shortest. If you can give me the proper reply, we can decide on a course of action."

Nick put his notebook on the bar counter, and squared his shoulders.

"Right. Fire away. Ask your question."

"What was El Greco's real name?" inquired H.M.

There was a pause.

H.M. was not fooling. Nick knew that. On the contrary, H.M.'s serious expression was disturbing in its fixed purpose. Nick thought himself ready to answer most possible queries, but this left him floored. He stared back.

"Is this a catch? El Greco's name was El Greco, wasn't it?"

"Oh, my son! El Greco means 'The Greek.' You don't think his old man christened him that, do you?"

In the background, on a faintly yellow-lit stage, the square of the trap again showed open and black. Up through it, with steady and swift motion, rose the figure of Commander Dawson. He was still rising when he spoke.

"Was somebody," the Commander called out to them, "asking about El Greco's real name? That's as simple as volume so-and-so in an encyclopedia. His name was—"

"Haul the blighter down!" howled H.M., stung. "This is important. We got things to talk about. Haul the blighter down!"

A light showed beneath the trap, illuminating the Commander.

"What does he say?" Eleanor called from below.

"He says, haul me down!"

The Commander descended, looking diffident but puzzled.

Nick hesitated.

"I hope I haven't made a walloping fool of myself," he said. "But I don't see what El Greco has to do with this."

"No, son?"

"Or the gilded man either, if it comes to that. I submit, in all respect, that there's only one way the evidence can possibly work out. Let me give you a hint."

Nick mentioned the name of a character once very famous in fiction.

H.M., who had started to turn away, swung round again as though stuck with a pin.

"And I also admit," continued Nick, "that medical knowledge was never my strong point, or there's one bit of evidence I should have seen much sooner."

H.M. took a deep breath. "Yes, son. Yes. I sort of think you've got it now."

The feminine mind, as represented by Betty, is often fond of puzzles. But a continuous series of cryptic remarks, made in her hearing by two bland-speaking persons sharing a secret, can drive a woman nearer to distraction than almost any cause except a blighted love affair or a husband's wearing of an objectionable hat.

Betty was more patient than most. But she apeared to be getting towards her limit. Looking from one to the other of them, she clenched her hands tightly.

"You've tumbled to the point," inquired H.M., "about the blood on the adhesive tape?"

"Yes. Yes, I think so."

"And the scratched silver?" persisted H.M., extending a hand in the air as though pushing something.

"Oh, yes. That's definite."

"And the bruises round the head? They couldn't 'a' been anything else, could they? Hey?"

"Under the circumstances, no."

"Uh-huh. So you may get an idea of what I can do during a conjuring show, without once bein' suspected, which I couldn't do in private without bein' assaulted." H.M. spoke with an evil scowl. "This is only a theory yet, son. We got to prove it. If we do prove it—"

In the background, an enthusiastic group under the stage were still tinkering with the trap-door. This time it was the butler, Larkin, whom they shot up like a genie in a gray-and-gold grotto. Larkin directed an apologetic glance at the group by the bar, before he sank through the floor again.

Nick shook his head.

"I still don't see your game, sir." Masters's warning occurred to him. "Look here. There's not going to be any knife-throwing, or bullet-catching tricks, or anything like that?"

H.M. gave a ghoulish chuckle.

"Oh, son! No. This is no unmasking dodge. The person concerned won't guess anything about it. This is a straight entertainment which, I warn you, is goin' to be colossal."

"But—"

"Talk about it later. Burn it all, can't you at least gimme time to rehearse?"

Next to be whisked up through the trap-door was Vincent James, whom Eleanor had routed out from floors below. Vince did not give them time to lower him again. He stepped off the trap, alighted from the stage like a big cat, and strolled across to the bar. Wearing a blue double-breasted suit, and a carefully old tie in which the Hartonian colors were just visible, he made a figure of such unassuming elegance that Nick—standing by the bar with an untasted whisky in his hand—felt unshaven.

Vince looked down at him with tolerant friendliness, and touched the whisky glass.

"So early in the morning?" Vince queried. "My dear old boy. You'll be having delirium tremens next. Pour it out like a good fellow."

H.M. regarded Vince without any pleasure at all.

"I thought you said at dinner last night," glowered H.M., "that you were goin' to play squash this morning?"

"I was. There's a first-rate court in the garage."

"Well?"

"Young Dawson backed out. Funny thing, you know. I can't get that chap to play games for the life of me. And yet he was at Westminister. But it reminds me. Doctors."

"Doctors?" said H.M.

"Yes. I was thinking about it before I went to sleep last night. Doctors. I thought I ought to tell you that—"

H.M. was very gentle.

"Now see here, son. I got work to do. Would you kindly buzz off?"

"But don't you want to hear about it?"

"No!" said H.M.

"You're a queer old boy," mused Vince, meaning well. "You ought to do something about that corporation, you know. At your age, when you're so much past the prime of life, it can be dangerous. Probably drink too much port, too. By the way, don't mind if I'm critical of your conjuring show. No offense in it. It's just that these charity-do's always bore me, and I show it."

Again the trap-door opened, in a gush of light from below. Eleanor, coming up in search of Vince, made a scarlet-and-black figure with a smiling flash of teeth, her knees bent as though to jump.

At this point, too, occurred an interruption so unexpected that it shocked them all quiet. Betty Stanhope suddenly flung up the bar counter with a bang of wood against wood. She wormed out from behind it, hurried across the room, and ran out of the door.

"Excuse me," said Nick, and was after her instantly.

"Betty!" he called in the passage outside. "Betty!"

There was no reply.

The cupola at the top of Masque House formed an enclosure within an enclosure. The circular theater had no chink or window in its walls. But around it, a circle outside a circle, ran an outer enclosure formed at half-length windows. This made a passage, some three or four feet wide, which you could walk round like a promenade deck and take the sun if there happened to be any sun.

Nick glanced at the stairway leading down. It was uncarpeted, and he would have heard her if she had run down there.

"Betty!" he called again—and began to walk round the white-painted sun-porch with the straw matting underfoot.

It was cold here. Not freezing cold, but enough to make you

realize what lay outside. At intervals, a door among the windows led out to a flat attic roof now deep in snow.

"I'm quite all right," said a muffled voice. "Please go away!"

She was standing close to the windows, at the front, with her back towards him, and the crook of her elbow pressed over her eyes.

Betty spoke in a steadier voice.

"I really am all right," she insisted. "Only, if I had stayed there another second, I should have screamed. And I didn't want to do that."

Nick had the sense to keep quiet.

"First it was you and H.M.," said Betty. "Then all those people coming up through the trap-door. I couldn't decide whether this whole business is funny or horribly tragic."

After still another pause, she spoke again.

"Did you ever go, in the old days, to a silly exhibition in Montmartre, called Hell? Flavia's theater, that I've always been so fond of, just began to remind me of it. I half expected a stuffed snake on a string to come down from the ceiling and hiss at me."

Nick remained where he was, his hand on the inner wall.

They seemed up at a great height here. The edge of the attic roof, slightly sloping, fell away to the battlements of the walls-proper below. Then there was the smooth drop of rolling hills of snow, so white that they had taken on a bluish tinge. From where he stood, Nick could see both of the hollow and allegedly ornamental towers at the front.

"It was too hot in there," he said, clearing his throat. "Would you—er—like some air or something?"

He acted more as an outlet for violent emotion than because he thought she needed it. He went to one of the doors leading out on the roof, grasped the knob, and yanked. Though not locked, it was stuck; he tore it open amid a tinkle of small icy particles.

Betty dropped her arm and turned round. The fear in her face surprised him.

"For heaven's sake, don't go out there!"

"I wasn't going to. But why?"

"The roof looks flat. It isn't. It's safe enough in dry weather, but with ice or snow . . ."

Nick decided that she had had enough air. The blast whipped in, blowing her hair. Nick slammed the door, and it refused to catch. He slammed it again. He slammed it a third time; and the glass cracked across, shivered, and shredded with a collapsing

123

crash at his feet. But when he looked round, green with consternation, Betty was laughing.

It heartened him to see that laughter; to see the old expression fade out of her eyes, and the new, warm twinkle came back into them. She spread out her hands.

"I'm being the most ridiculous person in the world!" Betty cried. "Moods! Moods! Nothing but moods. There's nothing to be afraid of except my own imagination. Come on: let's go back. I must learn how to be the vanishing lady. I say, what sort of show *do* you think H.M. is going to give us this afternoon?"

18

"Ladies and gentlemen," began Commander Dawson. "Friends. Guests. And children."

Commander Dawson cleared his throat.

The sound made by a group of quiet children, which is that of a vast adenoidal breathing, lapped him round.

All were packed in. All had been scrubbed within an ace of godliness. The girls wore hair ribbons; the boys wore any variety of collar which, in the opinion of their parents, could inflict the most torture. Not a shoe in the house but creaked when walked in. From the solemn-eyed six-to-eight-year-olds in the front row, to the swaggering or self-conscious thirteens at the back, all were respectfully silent.

It was the custom to arrange them in rows according to sizes: except that in front of the first row of folding chairs, where the smallest children sat, an extra row had been put in to accommodate the large forms of Miss Clutterbuck, Sir John and Lady Minsterstroke, Major Babbage, Miss Durne, and Mr. and Mrs. Talbot. When a little girl offered the timid suggestion that she could not see, she was sharply told by Miss Clutterbuck not to be selfish.

The rector, a saner man, sat at the back to keep his eye on a rowdy choir.

Standing at the back, too, were lined up the servants at Waldemere under the eye of Mrs. Peters, the housekeeper.

Perched on a stool inside the bar, which had been turned into a sort of box for household guests, Nick was crowded in with Christabel Stanhope, Dr. Clements, and Buller Naseby, with an extra stool for the Commander when his duties were finished. Eleanor and Vincent James were acting as stage managers, and Betty was the Great Kafoozalum's assistant.

124

These last four, at the moment, were not in evidence. The gray silk curtains were closed, and, in a dim mysterious glow, Commander Dawson stood before them.

"Ladies and gentlemen," he began for the second time. "Friends. Guests. And children."

The Commander cleared his throat again.

"What I mean to say is." he pursued, sticking his hands into his pockets and immediately taking them out again, "that at this festal season of the year it is meet that we should wish each other festal greetings: you know what I mean?"

"Hear, hear!" applauded Major Babbage piously.

Miss Clutterbuck also applauded.

The children remained respectfully but stolidly silent.

Most of them had left home with a festal clip over the ear, and instructions to behave themselves or expect reprisals. Under the eye of Miss Clutterbuck, they had trudged half a mile or more through the first real snow of the year, without being so much as allowed to stick each other's heads in it. On arriving at Waldemere, they had been told that there was "a very ill person" upstairs: that they must walk on tiptoe and speak in whispers.

This is bad for the mental balance. Toes were beginning to wriggle inside creaky shoes. Fingers tugged at collars, a universal gesture. Under plastered hair, ideas churned. Indeed, anybody but a Child Psychologist would have seen that this bottling-up presaged signs of explosion in a first-class beano.

"These festal—festal greetings," pursued Commander Dawson, "I now heartily offer you on behalf of our hostess, Mrs. Dwight Stanhope, in the hope that you will all join in the f-fun and enjoy the many surprises which the afternoon will no doubt bring forth."

"Hear, hear!" said the gruff voice of Major Babbage.

"Hear, hear!" said Miss Clutterbuck.

"But I will no longer delay you with fiscal greetings from the feast of mystery which is to be spread before us."

("And a jolly good thing too," whispered Christabel, almost against Nick's ear. "Why ever did you make poor Pinkey deliver the introductory speech?")

("Eleanor insisted.")

"Our guest this afternoon is that famous entertainer known throughout Europe and America as the Great Kafoozalum. The Great Kafoozalum is—" here Commander Dawson consulted his notes—"a real Hindu."

"Of course," confided Miss Clutterbuck, in a loud stage-whisper, "everybody knows it's only Sir Henry Merrivale."

"He has studied among the Yogi of India and the Lamas of Thibet. His powers have amazed the world. Your eyes shall see great wonders. Magic portents shall descend from the sky. Ladies and gentlemen, guests and friends . . . The Great Kafoozalum!"

Commander Dawson climbed down off the stage, and crept away.

The silk curtains flew apart as though blown by a sort of silent explosion. They disclosed a black-draped stage set with silvery single-legged tables, together with other apparatus confused and confusing. And the Great Kafoozalum himself strode confidently forth.

"My word!" said Sir John Minsterstroke.

Christabel took one look; then she pressed her hands over her face and began to rock helplessly back and forth.

Nick also looked. And, though he had been steeling himself against something pretty horrible, still he could not help recoiling.

It is customary to speak of evening clothes as "flawless." Now, the Great Kafoozalum's evening clothes were not flawless. They might have been criticized by a Savile Row tailor. But at least they were evening clothes. His white waistcoat was recognizable as a waistcoat. His shirt front did not unduly bulge. His trousers stayed up.

Nor could anybody have found fault with the great black cape, lined with scarlet, which swung from his shoulders, or the white gloves on his hands. The esthetic fault lay in other matters.

On his head the Great Kafoozalum wore a huge bulging turban, fastened in front with a single paste ruby, from which a tall white aigrette rose up like the radio antennae of a police car. From beneath this, a broad chocolate-brown face, ornamented by shell-rimmed spectacles, glared out with indescribable malignancy. From his face sprouted a bristling black beard, a monarch among beards, which extended up to his ears in one majestic fan.

And at last there was a response from the children.

Across the theater rolled that sudden, spontaneous murmur of "*Oooh!*" which is the sign of impressed admiration. He might have stepped straight out of a picture book. And the children knew it.

"What a *clever* make-up!" said Miss Clutterbuck. "Of course, children, you know it's *only* a make-up?"

The Great Kafoozalum stopped short, and looked at her.

126

"Can you see, Doris? Can you see, Annabel? Can you see, Margery?"

"Please, ma'am: no, ma'am."

"Now don't be nasty, ungrateful little girls! Sit quiet and I'll tell you how the gentleman does his tricks."

The Great Kafoozalum looked at her again.

But he resumed his march. Preceded by his corporation, he strode towards what should have been the footlights.

Behind him followed Betty, ethereal in a white frilled evening gown against the dark curtains. With a lordly gesture, the stumping figure in the black beard unslung his cape, took it off, and threw it back to her. He raised his gloved hands, moving the wrists and fingers; and, as he stripped off the gloves, they vanished into thin air.

Unfortunately, the Great Kafoozalum took one stride too far.

The turban with the aigrette left his head, rose gracefully into the air, and appeared to float sideways some two feet.

It was like an invitation. As though by collaboration with the powers of heaven, a large and heavily weighted motion-picture screen fell from above like a magic portent descending from the sky, and conked the Great Kafoozalum squarely on top of his bald head.

"God damn it to hell!" said a female voice from back-stage. The theater was noted for its fine acoustics.

There was a terrible silence. Miss Clutterbuck rose from her chair, turned round, fixed every child in that audience with her eye, and dared anybody to laugh.

Now this says much for the power of Miss Clutterbuck's eye. When growing youth, in successive seconds, (a) sees a full-grown adult stand under a weighted screen and cop a ninepenny one, and (b) hears some of the ripest of forbidden words used in front of the parson, the result is automatic.

Indeed, a sort of shiver went through the theater. The younger children remained solemn-eyed and fascinated, remembering. A twelve-year-old at the back, doubled up in a silent paroxysm like cramp, had to be led out. Several of the servants had slid down the wall, their heads buried in their arms.

As for the Great Kafoozalum himself, many British pugilists might have taken lessons from him. He was groggy but game. At the moment, since the white screen still dangled down in front of him, little could be seen of him except a pair of swaying legs.

127

But, when the screen jerked upwards, he stood in a grimly lofty attitude, commanding it to heaven. As he stepped backwards, the turban—its polite work now finished—floated back and settled on his head.

"Jolly good show, what?" exclaimed Major Babbage.

Fixing his audience with a murderous scowl, and pressing his turban firmly if somewhat skew-wiff on his head, the Great Kafoozalum now got down to business. Still he had not spoken a word. He went through a rapid routine, not badly, with colored handkerchiefs. Then he held up and exhibited to the audience a huge bowl of clear glass.

This bowl the Great Kafoozalum placed on a table. He took up a pitcher and sloshed water into it, half full. Then he beckoned to Betty, who approached unsteadily carrying a large tray on which were heaps of colored sand: red, blue, and yellow.

The Great Kafoozalum pushed up his sleeves to the elbows. Seizing double handfuls of colored sand, he flung them into the water and stirred them there. He kept whirling his arms round as he did this, spilling sand and making a noble mess which went straight into the spectator's hearts. When the concoction in the bowl looked sufficiently repulsive, he made a commanding gesture.

"*Ya Allah!*" said the Great Kafoozalum.

He plunged his hands, one after the other, into the water. He fished out handful after handful of various-hued sands, which he proceeded to fling about or pour out on the carpet—perfectly dry.

The first slow scattering of applause grew to thunder.

Miss Clutterbuck was frigidly amused.

"Can you see, Doris?"

"Yes, Miss Clutterbuck, God damn it to hell."

"A favorite of dear Mr. Maskelyne thirty years ago," said Miss Clutterbuck in a piercing voice which carried all over the theater. "The secret . . . did you speak, Doris?"

"No, ma'am, please."

"The secret," said Miss Clutterbuck, "lies in small water-proofed bags of paper or fish-skin, which contain dry sand. They are conveyed to the bowl under cover of double-handfuls of loose sand, and the muddy water prevents our seeing them. The conjuror has only to pick them out and burst them in his hand, letting the sand run out, after which he returns the bag to the water under cover of his palm."

The Great Kafoozalum stopped, and looked at her again.

"Ha, ha ha," yodeled Miss Clutterbuck.

A close observer might have noted that the Great Kafoozalum's foot was slowly tapping the floor.

But no other expression crossed his horrible face.

He waddled over to the wings, and with one hand led out Eleanor. He marched her with immense dignity across the stage. Eleanor, in light blue, looked at the audience and giggled foolishly.

The Great Kafoozalum held up for inspection an ordinary-looking light wooden chair. He then held up a copy of *The Times,* which he spread out on the stage to show that there were no trap-doors, and set the chair on top of it.

Eleanor was placed in the chair. After a fierce whispered conversation with her, in which each gestured at the other like a pair of Hebrew comedians, the Great Kafoozalum exhibited an immense cloth of crimson silk. After whirling this round him like the late Isadora Duncan, he draped it over Eleanor so that it fell to the floor, concealing Eleanor and chair.

"I say, you know—what?" whispered Major Babbage.

"What?" inquired Sir John Minsterstroke, coldly.

"Jolly good show," said the major. "Good gad alive!" he added, as though stung.

"Ooooh!" breathed the younger element, in one powerful adenoidal exhalation of breath.

"Well, I never!"

"Dod dammit it ell!"

The effect, Nick had to admit, was honestly startling. He gave the old man full marks. After some preliminary hocus-pocus, the Great Kafoozalum merely seemed to reach out and point to the cloth. There was the chair. There was *The Times.* But Eleanor, and the crimson cloth which had concealed her, both simultaneously vanished like a soap-bubble.

This time there could be no doubt about the volume of the applause. It nearly took the roof off. It was not merely appreciation of the trick: it was one mighty outlet for other bottled-up emotions. Thirteen-year-old boys were observed to stand up and scream at the top of their lungs.

An expression of something like serenity spread across the Great Kafoozalum's unmentionable face. He approached the audience, and bowed as low as his corporation would permit.

"That," said Miss Clutterbuck, "was Baultier de Kolta's 'Vanishing Lady,' as improved by Charles Bertram."

The Great Kafoozalum froze.

"Its secret," said Miss Clutterbuck, "lies mainly in the chair. This is so constructed that wires can be raised from its frame to

129

show the outline of head, shoulders, arms, and knees. The seat folds open. The newspaper is not really uncut, as you think."

The Great Kafoozalum lowered his head a little. His fingers, raised to shield his eyes, started to tap on his forehead.

Christabel Stanhope was almost weeping.

"It would be perfectly all right," she muttered, "if it weren't for that dreadful woman. Can't you do something about it, Inspector?"

"I'm not sure," said Nick, "that it will be necessary."

"Not necessary?"

"No. If your Miss Clutterbuck goes on like this, something tells me in a loud, clear voice that she is going to cop a packet."

"When Eleanor Stanhope sat in the chair," pursued Miss Clutterbuck, "and the cloth thrown over her hid her from you, the wires were raised. She could then slip down through the chair, through the doctored newspaper, and through the trap-door, while you thought you saw her head and body outlined through the cloth. This framework can be made to collapse at the proper time. As for disappearing cloth, dear Mr. Bertram used to—"

Enough is enough. Suddenly, with galvanized motion, the Great Kafoozalum removed the turban from his head, hurled it violently on the floor, and jumped on it. Though not a calculated effect, this produced almost as much applause as the vanishing lady.

"I say, what's he up to now?" whispered Major Babbage. "Is he goin' to make it jump up and bite him this time?"

Christabel spoke pleadingly.

"Sir Henry, no! For heaven's sake, no!"

Somewhere, somehow, the Great Kafoozalum managed to clutch at his sanity and get a grip on himself. After breathing deeply a few times, he caught up the turban and crammed it on. It had been somewhat bashed about, the aigrette now slanting at an angle of forty-five degrees. If he still resembled an Eastern potentate, he resembled an Eastern potentate just returning from the harem after an argument with one of his more temperamental wives.

"Ladies and gentlemen," intoned the Great Kafoozalum, in a deep guttural voice.

Instantly there was dead silence.

The Great Kafoozalum took a deep breath.

"As I was walkin' down the Strand the other day," he said, beginning a bit of that patter which no conjuror can resist, "as I was walkin' down the Strand the other day, I met a friend of mine, Mr. Ernest Bevin. He said to me—"

"Wot about the Indian rope-trick?"

It must not be thought that any such query came from Mr. Bevin. It came from the chauffeur, standing at the back with his arms folded.

The Great Kafoozalum shut his eyes.

"You said you could do the Indian rope-trick. What *I* say is: O.K. Let's see it."

"Well, really!" said Miss Clutterbuck, stiffening.

"The gentleman," said the Great Kafoozalum, "would like to see the Indian rope-trick."

"And so should I," declared Miss Clutterbuck. "But I must say, Mrs. Stanhope, that the license which seems permitted to the lower orders in this house—"

The Great Kafoozalum stroked his mighty beard.

"And the lady," he said, "would also like to see the Indian rope-trick. Hey?"

"My dear sir, I beg you not to be perfectly ridiculous. There is no such thing."

"No?"

"No, of course not."

The Great Kafoozalum adjusted his spectacles. Putting one hand on his waistband in front, and one on the back, he hitched up his trousers like a sailor. Squaring his shoulders, and assuming a hideously winning expression like that of Blackbeard the Pirate welcoming the officers of a captured Spanish galleon, he leaned forward and held out his hand.

"Step right up, madam," he invited.

"Are you sure this is all right?" whispered Christabel.

"I'm dead certain it's not," said Nick.

"As far as I'm concerned," returned Christabel, viewing the grains of colored sand adhering to the Great Kafoozalum's beard, "he can do what he likes to the old witch. I hope he does. But—"

"Inspector Wood!"

"Really—" Miss Clutterbuck began icily.

"Inspector Wood!"

"Go on, Emma," roared Major Babbage, giving her a violent dig in the ribs with his elbow. "Be a sport. Step up."

"Inspector Wood!"

At last Nick became aware of the insistent mutter which had been coming from somewhere behind his ear.

Abruptly he realized that he and Christabel were alone inside the miniature bar. When the others had slipped away he had not noticed. Behind him, in a strained and rigid attitude, stood

131

Larkin. The overhead lamp in the bar was on: and Larkin's face, though composed, showed white and damp.

"I beg your pardon, madam. Sir, may I have a word with you? It's rather urgent."

Always the same. Always, when you take it easy or let your mind run down in contentment, something breaks through to shatter it. Christabel craned her head round, and shushed Larkin.

"Nothing wrong, is there?" Christabel whispered, consulting her wrist-watch. "It's half-past four. Tea for the children at five?"

"Yes, madam. It is all prepared. Will you come this way, sir?"

The dim, crowded theater was intensely hot.

Nick had not noticed it until he groped out after Larkin. From the stage, H.M. was saying something about asking a few gentlemen to step forward as well. But Nick did not catch it. Larkin was ahead, holding open the door.

Outside, the chill of the sun-deck struck through Nick's clothes. Twilight was coming down: it made the white paint of the passage seem lighter and more luminous than the sky. Nick carefully closed the door against a gust of laughter which burst and rang against the padded walls.

"Well?" he prompted. "Did you do as I told you? Have you had the laundry-marks compared?"

"Yes, sir. They're Mr. Stanhope's. But—"

It was an unnerving business to see the man's composure completely break, to see nerves bubbling underneath. Larkin's face became an ugly seasick color. He had to put one hand on a white window ledge to steady himself.

"What is it, man? *What's wrong?*"

"It's Mr. Stanhope," answered Larkin. "He's dead."

19

"I tell you, he can't have had a relapse!" Nick shouted, after so long a pause that they seemed to have been there for minutes. "He was all right this morning! He was all right a few hours ago!"

"It wasn't a relapse," said Larkin.

They looked at each other.

"Someone's at it again," Larkin continued. "Someone came in and smothered him with a pillow while he was asleep."

Moving, smoky clouds drifted outside the circle of windows. Despite padded walls, another burst of laughter rang from inside the theater. One part of Nick's mind told him that this was what he had been fearing all along, so that he could neither rest nor let anyone else rest.

"But what about the people who were to watch? Hamley—and that other fellow? He wasn't supposed to be left alone for as much as a second."

Larkin let go the window ledge and straightened up.

"Hamley's sound asleep. In the chair, snoring, with his mouth open." Larkin made a bothered gesture, as though shielding his eyes. "How could I tell? He kept saying he was tired. But I didn't think he could be that tired. Some of these fellows will do anything to dodge honest work. That's my experience."

"Who found him?"

"I did, sir."

"When?"

"Just now."

A sick kind of despair settled on Nick. The realization of what this would mean was creeping into every corner of his mind: was penetrating, after the first shock, to his heart and conscience.

Well, but could he have prevented it? Yes, if he had sat by Stanhope's bed himself, every second of the forty-eight hours. Otherwise, no. And that wouldn't have been very practicable. All the same, it was nauseating medicine.

Stanhope wasn't Betty's own father, true. But—

"At least," he heard Larkin's voice going at a kind of dim buzz, "I think he was smothered. And there's one other thing, sir, that makes me think the murderer must be a lunatic. Stark mad crazy as a loon. Will you come and see?"

No other person seemed to move in Masque House as they jostled each other down three long flights of stairs.

Hollow as a mask without a face. Empty.

The door of Dwight Stanhope's bedroom stood wide open. Nick could hear Hamley snoring even before they reached it.

Against dusk, the brass lamp in the corner threw stronger beams, bringing out the pattern of the carpet. In his usual wing chair, Hamley sat with one leg hooked over the side, his back slumped, his chin on his breast, and his head sometimes agitated by the rattle of his own snores.

Dwight Stanhope lay much as Nick remembered from this morning, except that his arms were now flung out wide, and only one pillow was beneath his head.

133

The other pillow was lying near his hand. About the body showed few evidences of a physical struggle. The arch of the neck, maybe. The color of the face. The slight disarrangement of the eiderdown, as by a foot suddenly kicked downwards in convulsion. But what took the eye first was one single grotesque detail.

On the dead man's breast, somebody had placed a saucer full of water.

Nick looked quickly at the bedside table. He had a vivid remembrance of seeing there, this morning, two medicine bottles standing in a saucer, and a cut-glass pitcher of water. The saucer was no longer there. It rested on Stanhope's chest; the lamplight lay on a sheen of water that was as quiet as the chest, while another snore from the sleeping Hamley gurgled out, startlingly, and died away.

"That's what I mean," Larkin muttered. "That saucer."

"Yes. You say you found him—when?"

"Just before I came upstairs to get you."

Nick consulted his watch.

"About four-thirty, say? That'll do well enough. How did you happen to come in here?"

Larkin's broad mouth tightened. "I heard *him* snoring, sir. That's how. The house was as quiet as a tomb and you couldn't help but hear. There's one other thing. As I put my hand on the knob of the door, here, I could have sworn I heard somebody running."

"Footsteps?"

"Yes, sir."

"Running where?"

"Hard to say. Towards the dressing room, maybe?" It was a doubtful question rather than the statement. Larkin turned his eyes on the dressing-room door. He shook a grizzled, close-cropped head.

"But you didn't see anybody?"

"No, sir."

Nick went over to the bed. The man who was killed twice. No doubt about his being dead this time. Nick lifted one eyelid, touched the nostrils, and noted, on the discarded pillow, the faint traces of blood from the nose. Suffocation, right enough. In Stanhope's present condition, it wouldn't have been difficult. From the wing chair, the sleeping Hamley emitted a snore of such choking, snorting quality that in a room of death it sounded obscene. Nick felt his nerves tingle with an uneasiness that swelled to wrath.

134

"For God's sake, wake him up! But turn him round and get him out of here before he notices this."

"Yes, sir."

"Don't pitch into him. Just find out what he knows, if anything. Also, see if you can find Dr. Clements. He was in the theater a while ago. And one thing more: don't mention this to anybody else, unless you can find Sir Henry Merrivale alone."

Hamley awoke with a fighting noise, like a half-dazed boxer doused in water. Larkin, that martinet to underlings, gave him a push in the back and impelled him out. Nick stared at the saucer of water on the dead man's chest—put there, of course, for a very good reason—and wondered about other things.

Why, *why* were murderers such damned fools?

Did they think themselves too clever to be caught? Or shut up their minds and trust to luck?

The irony was that this particular person had to go and choke a life out, smother a helpless man under a feather pillow, even after the police could prove against their quarry the attempted murder that failed. That, even all the offenses together, would only have meant penal servitude. Whereas this was a hanging matter. Did the murderer think the motive was worth it? Undoubtedly: to such a one, the motive would be overwhelming. But, visualizing the person whose wrists would be strapped together by the executioner, Nick felt his stomach turn sick inside him.

A voice said:

"Young man."

It spoke in a tentative way, as one who offers conciliation. Buller Naseby, wearing hat and overcoat, had come half way to the bed before Nick saw him. Mr. Naseby looked an old man, and himself a sick man.

"Young man. Excuse me. Is he . . .?"

"Yes. He's dead now."

"God help the poor fellow," said Mr. Naseby, and removed his hat. He was silent then, and Nick could think of no comment to make, until his companion spoke again. Mr. Naseby's face was screwed up into an expression of regret and real pity. But still another emotion sharpened his voice.

"What's that saucer of water doing on his chest?"

"Why do you ask, sir?"

"Don't fence with me," the other complained. His tone was shrill. "I'm tired. Don't fence with me all the time. What's that saucer of water doing on his chest? Did you put it there? No? Then why's it there?"

135

"I can understand your being interested," Nick told him. "This isn't the first time we've heard about a saucer of water. Wait! Before you deny it—" Mr. Naseby had opened his mouth—"think back to Thursday night. At going on for eleven, say. Where were you?"

"Up in the theater, with—him. Yes."

"That's right. You were eating potato chips out of a saucer at the bar. In fact, you finished them. Who came in? Eleanor Stanhope. What did she do, among other things? She went behind the bar to get herself a drink. She noticed the empty saucer. She . . . surely you must remember now?"

Mr. Naseby made a fierce, flagging gesture with his bowler hat.

In his mind Nick saw every detail, every color of that scene. He saw Eleanor, in white with pearls, snatch up the saucer and hold it under the water-tap. He saw her fill it to the brim and set it on the counter. Words still reverberated from the past. *"Do you know what that means?"* And, *"If I were dead—or dying—"*

Mr. Naseby tapped the rim of his bowler hat against his lower lip.

"Remembering's not understanding," he pointed out.

"No. But you do remember the words?"

"Why?"

"Because you may be asked to testify to them."

Mr. Naseby's eyes seemed to retreat into his head.

"Against that girl? Rubbish!"

"Not necessarily against anybody. Just that you heard them."

The other ignored this. "I was going home. I'll not go now. They may need me. This is horrible." He passed a hand down across the hair at the back of his head. "And I thought young Dwight was trying to steal his own pictures for the insurance! Should have known better. He always hated frauds and fakes."

"Yes," said Nick, "he did."

A noise from above interrupted them: a faint, stamping thunder, slowly drawing closer. Nick knew what it was. It was the advance guard of boys released, with a claustrophobic eagerness to get through the doors, and plunging downstairs, the show was over and he could count on only a few minutes more of grace.

Beckoning to Mr. Naseby, he went out into the hall and locked the door on the outside. They stood in the gallery at the head of the main stairs as the first wash of guests swept towards them. Rogers, Emory, and another footman whom Nick did not recognize stood in the hall below to stem and turn the tide.

136

But these boys were reasonably quiet. They were even hushed. Presently someone would begin to reminisce: then the voices would begin to talk faster and faster, and rise higher and higher, until they exploded like rockets. But at the moment they were still in the grip of illusion. Their flushed faces showed that rapt look which can be seen on the countenances of music-lovers leaving a Beethoven concert. One voice, expressing the general sentiment, rose from the group with a guardedness burgeoning into awe:

"Coo! Wasn't it super?"

Nobody replied.

The second wave was guided by the rector, Mr. Townsend, with an odd expression on his face.

But considerable traffic congestion was caused by the appearance of the third wave. For this contained H.M. himself, still in his costume of the Great Kafoozalum, with a small girl clinging tightly to either hand. The boys, though sneeringly disdaining such effete signs of friendship, nevertheless circled round and round him like Red Indians at a campfire, firing questions faster than newspaper reporters.

"Was it a trick when you dropped Miss Clutterbuck down the trap-door?"

"Why did you tie her up like that? Was it the Indian rope-trick?"

"And gag her?"

"Did she really have that bottle of gin in her handbag?"

"Why didn't she reappear again on top of the bar counter, like you said she was going to?"

"Well, now, son, I expect something went wrong with the spell. These tough old hyenas are pretty hard to put the hoodoo eye on. Just when you think you've got 'em, they slip away from you. I expect she's halfway home by now."

"Will you teach us how to put the hoodoo eye on people, so we can do it?"

"Crumbs, yes! Will you?"

"Where did you get all the ribbon you took out from under the man's waistcoat? Was it up your sleeve?"

But the girls would not be denied.

"Please, Mr. Kafoozalum, will you sign my autograph book?"

"And mine?"

"Sure, my dolly. But some other time. You go downstairs and get your ice cream and cake."

Please, Mr. Kafoozalum! It's awfully special!"

"All right, my dolly: Here you are. Now you cut along."

"Thanks awfully, Mr. Kafoozalum. Good-by."

The hall now rang with voices. H.M. stood at the head of the stairs, his fists on his hips, until the last of them had straggled down. Then he lumbered over to where Nick and Mr. Naseby stood.

"Did Larkin find you?" the former asked.

"Uh-huh. Looks as though I've sort of messed things up, don't it? Wait here. Back in half a tick."

He went down the side passage to his bedroom. When he returned five minutes later, all traces of the Great Kafoozalum had disappeared except the unwieldy evening clothes. He had an unlighted cigar in his mouth, and his face was bitter.

"You couldn't have prevented it!" Nick said.

"Well. And neither could you."

"That's what I tell myself," said Nick; "but I know I'm a liar. The one I should have watched wasn't Mr. Stanhope; it was the devil we're after. Afternoon! Entertainment! Every single witness safe upstairs. Guard dead for sleep. Ideal opportunity, and—just like that!" He snapped his fingers.

H.M. rolled the cigar round in his mouth.

"If it's any consolation to you, son, I proved up there what we wanted to prove."

"Ah! I thought you would. No doubt about it?"

"Not a ghost of a doubt, son."

"Then that completes it," said Nick. "I'm prepared to risk an arrest now, if you'll back me up."

H.M. nodded. Again he left them by the head of the stairs, and went to Dwight Stanhope's room. He unlocked the door, entered, was gone two minutes, and came out again. When he returned to the stairs his expression was even more dour and bitter.

"I'll back you up," he replied. "Y'know—" the cigar rolled in his mouth—"I said it might be tried, but who in the blazes thought it really *would* be tried. Well, that's that." His broad face smoothed itself out. "It's fitting, in a way. This afternoon I had the pleasure of riddin' the Stanhope family of a pest . . ."

"You mean the Clutterbuck?"

"I do. A pest, I repeat, of a sort that's rottin' England. So now we can get rid of another kind of pest that's nearly as common if not as dangerous in the same breed. A snake."

Buller Naseby, his bowler hat on again, stood motionless by the marble balustrade. Both H.M. and Nick appeared to have forgotten him. He cleared his throat.

"Have they heard—" he pointed—"up there?"

"No," said H.M.

138

"It will be bitter hearing."

"Sure it will. For one of them more than any other."

"Who's going to break the news?"

"Nobody's goin' to break the news," replied H.M., "as yet. We'll let 'em all work their feelings out on the business of the snake before they hear. By that time, there'll be an outlet. I hope."

"Young Dwight loved his family," said Mr. Naseby.

"Yes!" roared H.M., with extraordinary ferocity. He took the cigar out of his mouth and whacked his hand down on the balustrade. From below drifted an excited murmur of children's voices, filling and echoing in the marble hall.

"That's just it," said H.M. "He loved his family. He got killed because of it. If that close-mouthed beggar had taken anybody into his confidence, *anybody,* for a tenth of a second, he wouldn't be lyin' dead in there now. But the cat's been at the spilt milk. There's none left to weep over. C'mon, son. Better lock that door."

Mr. Naseby moistened his lips.

"You mean to have this out now?"

"That's the general idea."

The other made a stiff little gesture. "Sir, I am an old friend of the family—"

"Uh-huh. What's more, if it's been correctly reported to me, the most significant remark in this whole business was something Dwight Stanhope said to you on Thursday night. Like to come along and see the finish? By God, I warn you it *is* the finish."

Mr. Naseby hesitated only for a minute.

"I'll come," he said.

20

"Don't tell me," cried Christabel, "you've got rid of the Great Kafoozalum! I loved the Great Kafoozalum! His treatment of Miss Clutterbuck was masterly."

"Yes." Betty sounded worried. "But the woman got a most frightful bump. McGovern had to drive her home in the sleigh. She says she's going to sue H.M. for damages."

"She would," said Eleanor. "The old bitch got exactly what she deserved, and that's that."

"A propos," said H.M., in such a curious voice that they all stared at him, "there's somebody else I'd like to talk about, if you got time to spare."

Few persons now remained in the little theater.

Only the wall lamps burned yellow behind glass prisms, making a luminous dusk. The wilderness of folding chairs which cluttered its floor bore witness to invasion and exodus. Stray morsels of fruit and toffee would have to be dug out of the carpet. Somebody had lost a hair ribbon. The stage remained dark despite open curtains that showed a dim litter of conjuring apparatus.

In an armchair at the back lounged a pleased, glutted, exhausted Eleanor. Betty was tidying up the bar.

"Talk?" repeated Christabel. "Now? But I've got to go downstairs to the guests."

"Ma'am," said H.M., "I'd rather you didn't."

He went over and sat down on the edge of the stage, facing them. With a puzzled look, Christabel turned a folding chair towards him and hesitantly sat down.

No word had been spoken, no hint given. Yet three men, having heavy in their minds the color of a dead man's face downstairs, cannot enter a room without taking some breath of that atmosphere with them. H.M., Nick and Buller Naseby could not have avoided it if they had wished. H.M. said stolidly:

"Where are the others, ma'am?"

"What others?" cried Eleanor from the back. "Pinkey and Vince are repairing the trap-door lift. It got caught in Betty's dress, and it's stuck. Do you want them?"

"Presently," said H.M. "*You'd* better take a pew, Doctor."

Dr. Clements, noticeably pale against his cropped beard and mustache, hurried forward and stumbled over a folding chair. To the startled imaginations of most of those present, he seemed to have materialized out of the gray curtains on the wall.

"My dear Mrs. Stanhope," he began. "Nobody told me! I was given no opportunity to see—"

"Steady!" H.M. said sharply. "You'd better join us too son."

Round a corner of the stage, hitherto invisible, moved the apologetic figure of Larkin. A cough indicated his presence. He climbed clumsily down from the stage.

Betty, from behind the bar counter, spoke quietly.

"I know," she said. "Hell."

Christabel flung her head round.

"My dear, please don't swear. I've no objection to it, except that it doesn't become you. It's not your type."

"Actually," said Betty, pushing a saucer of potato chips to one side, "it wasn't swearing. Don't you remember the place

140

you and father took us to in Montmartre, when I was fifteen and Eleanor was eighteen? There wasn't the least thing wrong with it; but father hurried us out like a shot. It was called Hell. I said today that this place reminded me of it."

"Not a bad guess," observed Nick.

"What on earth *is* all this?" inquired Christabel, giving a bewildered glance round.

H.M. looked at her.

"Ma'am, when I tell you who tried to kill your husband—" in the shock of silence following, H.M. struck a match and lit his cigar—"certain persons here, maybe, are goin' to want my blood."

"So that's what's up," observed Eleanor.

"Nick!" cried Betty, and put out her hand. "Nick!"

He went to her instantly.

Christabel sighed. "Oh, Betty, Betty!" she said without inflection. "Betty, Betty, Betty!"

"They're going to say, maybe," pursued H.M., "that I'm a cloth-headed old fossil dodderin' towards senility and the House of Lords. So it's only fair for all of you to hear the evidence that Inspector Wood and I have gathered."

"Just a moment, please." Christabel turned her head. Her smile was one of the most attractive Nick had ever seen. "Mr. Wood. I wonder whether you'd mind if I asked you a very personal, rude, and even insulting question?"

"Not at all. Go ahead."

"What is your yearly income?"

Nick considered. "I can't give you details offhand, Mrs. Stanhope. It's three thousand pounds, more or less."

"Really? They must pay extraordinary salaries in the police force."

"It's not my salary," said Nick. "You must have guessed that from what Vince James told you. I'm sorry: I inherited it. It may seem like doing somebody out of a job; but you can't sit still and do nothing."

"Uh-huh. And that," said H.M. drowsily, "also enters into it."

"Does it?" said Christabel. "How?"

"Ma'am, yesterday you asked me two questions. First, why did your husband dress up as a burglar? Second, who stabbed him? I'm goin' to answer those questions, if you want to hear."

"Please go on."

H.M. was silent for a moment.

"To begin with, you'd better hear what Inspector Wood worked out for himself. Then I'll tell you what I'd already worked out. From two different directions, d'ye see. But converging, and fitting together. Like a mask and a face. Like a lock and a key."

H.M. took two puffs at the black cigar. He watched the smoke curl up against the dim gilt grotto of the stage above.

"Now, sort of throw your minds back to Thursday night. Or, if we got to be precise, to the early hours of Friday morning. The burglary occurs. Stanhope, in his fancy dress, is stabbed and kicked about by the sideboard.

"Inspector Wood finds him there. After a look at this very rummy situation, Inspector Wood asks Larkin to examine all the other door and window fastenings on the ground floor." H.M. opened one eye at Larkin. "What'd you find, son? Tell us."

The butler cleared his throat.

"Well, sir, all the doors were locked and bolted on the inside. All the ground-floor windows were locked on the inside."

H.M. nodded.

"That's right. Now kindly note the dining room. Outside the dining-room windows, there was a porch floor covered with light frost. In that frost there was one set of footprints—made by the burglar's tennis shoes—pointing inwards to the burgled window. No other marks! Nothing!

"D'ye see what it means? It means one thing. It means Stanhope didn't first walk out by one of those windows, and then turn round and walk back again. He couldn't have. Both windows were fastened on the inside. He approached from outside, leavin' the solitary footprints in the frost; he cut the window, turned the catch, and got in. Yes?"

"Yes," admitted Christabel.

"Well?" prompted H.M., sitting back and throwing out his hands. "Burn me, don't you see?"

"No."

"Then tell me," said H.M. *"how in blazes did Stanhope get out of the house to begin with?"*

There was a silence.

"An upstairs window . . . no, wait."

"An upstairs window?" repeated H.M. "Well, let's see. In your mind's eye, take a dekko at this house. It's got smooth, straight walls, without so much as a water pipe or a tendril of ivy on 'em. The ceilings of the rooms are fifteen feet high. Add a two-foot clearance between the floors. That's seventeen feet he's got to get down. How does he do it? Jump?"

Christabel cried out in alarm.

"Good heavens, no! Dwight's got—"

"He's got bones like glass," said Mr. Naseby sullenly. "Jump? Don't talk rubbish. He wouldn't even play running games. I told Inspector Wood so."

Again H.M. nodded.

"That's right. So it occurred to Inspector Wood, bang in the middle of the night, that a man like that wouldn't be likely to crawl out of a seventeen-foot window above iron-hard ground: even if he had a rope."

H.M. peered at Nick.

"It was a dizzyin' and upsetting sort of thought. Still, you can't tell. It'd have been an awful risk on Stanhope's part; but you can't tell. So the young feller there had to find out whether there might 'a' been a rope of any kind. He buzzed Larkin's telephone in the small hours, and Larkin said—"

The butler coughed.

"I said, sir, that I had examined the upstairs windows just after Mr. Stanhope was stabbed. There was no rope, or anything that could be used as a rope, hanging from any of them."

Nick pressed Betty's hand, which was lying across the bar-counter. The smoke of H.M.'s abominable cigar began to make itself felt on lungs and eyes in that close, stale air. From the back of the theater, Eleanor spoke with cynical weariness.

"See here, Homer. What are you getting at? If Pops couldn't get out of the house on the ground floor, and couldn't get out from the upper floor, then how in the name of sense *did* he get out?"

H.M. spread out his hands.

"He couldn't, my wench. He didn't."

"What?"

"We will now," announced H.M., drawing himself up with genteel modesty, and fixing them with a glare which dared them to contradict him, "we will now take me."

He tapped his own chest.

"I got to this house footsore, weary, and accursed. Oh, my eye. I felt somethin' of a cross between Charles the First on the scaffold and a dyin' duck in a thunderstorm. And in the servants' hall they told me something that couldn't possibly be true.

"Yet I was talking, mind you, to one of the blokes who'd carried Stanhope upstairs, undressed him, washed him, got him to bed, and shoved away his clothes in a wardrobe before the doctor came. He should have known, if anybody did."

H.M. blinked at Dr. Clements.

The tubby little doctor was sitting forward on the edge of a folding chair, staring at the carpet. His own expression had a twist of cynicism as he peered up.

"Next," pursued H.M., "let's take the stab wound in Stanhope's chest. Looky here, Doctor. I'll run over the points about that wound as you outlined 'em to Inspector Wood. Just tell me if I'm correctly statin' 'em, will you?"

"I am at your service, sir."

"Good. It was a straight, deep incision, made by a wafer-thin blade four or five inches long?"

"Correct."

"Uh-huh. And the danger to Stanhope's life was from interior bleeding?"

"It was."

"The lips of the wound were so compressed that at first you had trouble findin' the wound at all? You said that, didn't you?"

"I did."

"Is that a fairly common kind of wound, now?"

"Reasonably so, given a very thin blade."

"Uh-huh. We're nearly there. Tell me, Doctor. What's the chief characteristic of wounds like that?"

A faint, sour smile twisted Dr. Clement's bearded mouth. His eye ran round the group.

"There is no exterior bleeding," he replied.

Nick had been waiting for his. He had been wondering, watching, calculating its effect. Even so, he was not prepared for the stunning shock with which the blow took them. It took perhaps ten seconds before most of those in the group realized what Dr. Clements had said. There was a small rattle as Christabel Stanhope knocked over the folding chair in getting to her feet.

"No exterior bleeding?" Christabel almost screamed. "Are you mad?"

"No," said H.M.

"But that was the most horrible part of it!" cried Eleanor. "I mean, we saw him lying there with his blood all over the coat and the shirt and the trousers and—"

"Oh, no, you didn't," said H.M.

"The man really is loopy," Eleanor said wildly, and got up.

"You didn't see *his* blood," H.M. explained with patient care. "You saw somebody else's blood."

H.M.'s cigar had gone out. He lit it again, the spurt of the match flame yellow and vicious against the dim stage. Then the red end of the cigar began to glow.

"See here," he went on. "It's very simple. I knew there was something fishy when I heard about a wound that didn't agree

144

with the slappin' big quantity of blood. But the wound was there. And the blood was there, and I got Nick Wood to show me the clothes.

"In justice to Dr. Clements, *he* never saw the clothes at all. He never saw Stanhope till Stanhope was washed and abed. So he saw nothing rummy to report. It looked like a wound that hadn't bled outwardly; and it was.

"I told you yesterday that the answer to this business could be given in two words. Those words are, 'He didn't.'

"How did Stanhope get out of the house? He didn't. Why did Stanhope, who hated masquerade, dress himself up in burglar's clothes? He didn't. Burn it all, don't you see that *the murderer changed clothes with the victim?*"

H.M. adjusted himself more comfortably on the edge of the stage.

"Mr. Buller Naseby," he said.

"I beg your pardon?" shrilled Mr. Naseby.

"When you were talking to Dwight Stanhope up here in this theater on Thursday night, and tryin' to interest him in your gilded-man proposition . . ."

"Yes?"

"Did he say to you, 'There's only one gilded man I'm after?' "

"Why?"

"Never mind that. Did he?"

"Yes, he did."

"Did you understand what he meant?"

"No."

"That's a pity," said H.M., with a slow and dismal shake of his head. "That's an awful pity. It might 'a' saved a lot of trouble if you had."

"Gilded man?" screamed Christabel. "What are you raving about now? What gilded man?"

"After all, d'ye see," H.M. said reflectively, "there's only one person it could be."

A voice, somewhere, triumphantly said, "Got it!" But who spoke, or even where the words came from, few persons in that group could have told you. The words might have come from the theater or under it. But all of them noticed the light. It gleamed out on the dim stage behind H.M.'s motionless bulk. It wavered up into the grotto as he spoke.

"There's only one person," continued H.M., "whose clothes would have fitted Dwight Stanhope. There's only one person as tall as Stanhope, and of just his build. Oddly enough, Stanhope was once actually mistaken for this person, when seen from behind, in this very room on Thursday night."

145

"It is Hell," said Betty. "It really *is* Hell!"

"The trap-door's coming up," said Christabel.

"So it is," agreed H.M., his voice rumbling out with a kind of ferocious tenderness. "And, also oddly enough, the feller in question is payin' us a visit at this very minute. That's the gilded man, my fatheads. That's the murderer."

The trap, smooth-slipping on its oiled cogs, worked not quite so swiftly as usual. It distorted the light as it moved. They saw the head, they saw the shoulders, they saw the body, they saw the legs. And, as the head came up while H.M. was speaking, that light caught other things—things about the eyes, for example—that were usually seen in the pleasant face of Vincent James.

21

Did you call me?" asked Vince.

The trap-door had closed, and he stood again in half dusk.

"In a way," said H.M. "You'd better come down here, son. They'll be takin' you along to the police station presently."

Nick was watching Eleanor at the back. He alone saw Eleanor jump up and hurry across to the panel of electric switches. But they all saw the lights that illuminated Vince on the stage.

Eleanor had about her a kind of diabolical inspiration. You might have believed, then, that she could see through the features into the brain. Her right hand was on the switches, her left pressed hard just under her left breast, and you could hear her breathe. She studied Vince. She studied him again, with moving eyes.

Vince had begun to laugh very heartily, but he stopped.

"It's true," Eleanor said. "I felt there was something. But I couldn't guess what. By God, it *is* true."

"Look here, what's the joke?" asked Vince—and took a step back.

"There's no joke, son," murmured H.M.

"No, Vince, it's true," said Nick. "I'm taking you along."

"What's the charge?"

"Murder."

Betty's elbow, moving involuntarily, swept the saucer of potato chips off the bar counter. They fell at Buller Naseby's feet, but he did not volunteer to pick them up.

146

"You mean attempted murder," corrected Christabel, trying to speak lightly. "If this is true, that is."

"True?" said Vince. "True?"

Nick studied him. Nick thought: For the first time in his life, this bloke's been caught at something. It's a new experience. He doesn't know what to make of it.

Vince was smiling the old, pleasant, tolerant smile. His tight-curling light hair, the unobtrusive cut of his dark blue suit, the good structure of forehead and nose and chin, were all subtly contradicted by that expression about the eyes.

"I don't get this," he declared, shaking his head in a puzzled way. "I may not be very bright, but—"

"Oh, son!" said H.M., in a dispirited way. "You've been dinning that into people's ears for so long that they believe you. What price the Cataract House emeralds? What price the Pensbury Old Hall Leonardo? And you're bright enough when you're with a woman, because you can't resist showing off. No, son. You're too clever by half."

Christabel abruptly drew out another chair, and sat down.

"Indeed, old boy?" observed Vince, with that mild arrogance which was like a blow in the face. "And what am I supposed to have done?"

"Do you want me to tell them all about it, son?"

"Suit yourself, pop."

"Then it's like this. Eleanor Stanhope—"

"Just a moment," interrupted Christabel. "Larkin. I think you'd better leave us."

"Yes, madam."

"I imagine you have learned how to hold your tongue?"

"Yes, madam."

"Go on, Sir Henry."

"Eleanor Stanhope," pursued H.M., "had fallen violently in love with a man whom her father knew to be a fraud and a fake. That's the whole sad story in one sentence."

Christabel got up, but sat down again.

"Look at him," said H.M., making a casual gesture towards Vince. "Is there anybody he reminds you of? Can you think of any schoolboy hero of his that he's been modelin' himself after, line for line?"

"I think—"

"Ever hear of Raffles, the Amateur Cracksman?" asked Nick.

"In my younger days," continued H.M. "when we took our stories seriously, there was one character I could never stand at any price. That was Raffles. He put my back up every time I

147

tried to read about him. What beat me was why we were supposed to regard the feller as a gentleman.

"Raffles, you may remember, was a great cricketer and no end of a social swell. On the strength of his cricket, he would be invited to a country house. There he would pinch what swag he liked; and justify himself because the person he robbed was so plebeian. We were supposed to applaud the debonair, great-hearted chap who robbed the rich in order to give to A. J. Raffles, and say hoo-roar.

"But let's leave fiction out of this. There are people like that in real life. They feel they're socially born to the purple. If they haven't got money, they feel they've got a right to take it. And then they're right and everybody else is wrong.

"That beauty in front of you—" H.M. pointed with his cigar—"makes his livin' as a professional crook. If that hurts his feelings, I'll say amateur crook. He's invited everywhere. He knows every inch of half the big houses in England. He knows what's valuable, and who's got it, and how to approach it.

"He's not such a fathead, as a rule, as to lift a string of emeralds from another guest while he's actually staying *in* the house. But an outside job will do just as well. Two or three good hauls a year will keep him in clover. And here's the beauty of his procedure: that an outside job is made to look like an inside job, and an inside job like an outside job. Which is why, because of the different technique, that Inspector Wood didn't at first spot him as the burglar of Pensbury Old Hall and Cataract House.

"If, for instance, he's marked down a little item by Leonardo da Vinci . . ."

"Hold on, governor," urged Vince.

His massive astonishment was as convincing an expression as Nick had seen.

"If I'm supposed to have done something, you'd better tell me what it is. Who's Leonardo What-is-it? Dago, I take it. What does he do?"

"Son," said H.M., with a critical air, "don't you think that's a bit overdone? You always seem to be goin' out of your way to insist, over and over, how little you know or care about painting. Don't you protest too much?"

"No. It's true."

"Uh-huh. Then you wouldn't happen to know El Greco's real name?"

"Not unless it's El Greco, no."

"I was just wondering," said H.M. in a brooding tone, "how many people could announce, offhand, in ringin' tones, that the name of the Cretan Spaniard called The Greek was Domenico

Theotocopulo. It's a very rummy thing that in the billiard room yesterday, when you were honestly puzzled and off-guard, you walloped out with, 'What's old Domenico got to do with it?' A propos of the El Greco picture.

"However, we won't press that. What we will say is that Dwight Stanhope tumbled to you."

H.M. paused.

"How he tumbled to you we're probably never goin' to learn . . ."

"Until Dwight wakes up, of course," corrected Christabel.

"Yes," said H.M. slowly, "until Dwight wakes up."

There was a bursting quality about the silence which made Nick want to look anywhere but at Christabel or Eleanor. H.M. himself was so distressed that he could not look at them either, but glared at the floor and puffed violently at his cigar.

Vincent James strolled across the stage, leaned against the arch, and smiled.

H.M. cleared his throat, not without effort.

"Well! And Eleanor, the particular apple of Dwight's eye, had fallen head over heels for this fraud and fake.

"He hated fakes, y'know. But Dwight didn't say to her, 'Look here, girl, this chap's a wrong un; and I'll tell you why.' In this particular case I think he was wise. The gal might not have believed him. Or, without seein' the chap's plain meanness for the ugly thing it is, she might have regarded him as a kind of romantic Robin Hood.

"Dwight Stanhope was just as patient and just as close-mouthed as always. His behavior didn't vary. He wasn't goin' to tell Eleanor. He was goin' to *show* her. He was goin' to—"

"To set a trap," breathed Christabel.

H.M. nodded.

"'Will you walk into my parlor?'" quoted Nick. There floated in front of him a picture of Dwight Stanhope's face.

"What was that, Inspector Wood?"

"Let it go, Mrs. Stanhope. Only something your husband once said. Go ahead, H.M. This is your show—up to a point."

Again H.M. nodded; the corners of his mouth turned down.

"Bull's eye, ma'am. To set a trap, with a police officer in the house. He brings down the most valuable paintings, from a gallery wired with burglar-alarms to an unprotected ground-floor room. Bait! He himself starts all those mysterious rumors, widely circulated among his friends, that he's gettin' very hard up. More bait!

"Thinks Master Vincent James, 'Oh? So that's it. The old boy's nearly broke. He'd like to see those pictures stolen, eh, to get the insurance? Good! Why shouldn't *I* oblige?' Which, d'ye see, was exactly what Dwight wanted him to think.

"So our modern Raffles comes down here, prepared for an inside job which is goin' to look just like an outside job.

"His clothes? Old stuff, used in other raids. All ready-made, unmarked things that can't be traced even if he should lose some of it. Burglars often have the nasty luck of bein' compelled to leave a cap, or a coat, or even a pair of shoes behind. But these things? They won't be noticed even by the valet who unpacks. Old tweed cap and coat? Only natural. Corduroy trousers? It's likely to be skiing weather. Tennis shoes in winter? Certainly: isn't there a first-rate squash court in the garage?"

Eleanor, still by the light switches, laughed. And Christabel flung her head round.

"Do you find this so funny, darling?"

"No, darling," returned Eleanor. "I was just thinking."

"Thinking what?"

"That the dear boy's ardor for me," said Eleanor, "started to cool off as soon as he must have heard father was hard up." Then, quietly, she began to cry.

"Ma'am!" roared H.M., so strangled with embarrassment that the cigar nearly flew out of his hand. "Miss! Gal! Oi!"

"Go on, Sir Henry," said Christabel. "Come to the burglary on the famous night."

H.M. seized at the opportunity.

"At about three o'clock in the morning, our Mr. James got ready." H.M. peered at Nick. "Where's his bedroom?"

"His bedroom," answered Nick, "is at the back of the house, on the first floor, just over the dining room. It's next to mine, connecting by way of a bathroom."

"Uh-huh. Over the dining room. And what is there hooked to the window in each of the bedrooms, son?"

"A Southerby Patent fire-escape rope."

"Easy meat," said H.M. "He gets into his outfit, and shins down the rope, leavin' it against the side of the house. I'm told he always keeps both windows wide open at night. He prowls round the garden. If anybody in that place does happen to be awake, and sees a ghosty shadow, it'll be remembered later as double stress on the illusion that the burglar came from outside.

"All's well. Up he goes, at a quarter-past three, cuts the dining room window, slips in, snaffles the El Greco, and starts to cut it out of the frame. But there's just one lttle thing he hasn't calculated on.

"Dwight Stanhope is waiting for him."

H.M.'s gesture conjured up, with intolerable vividness, the dark dining room; the little electric torch propped across the sideboard in a single beam of light; the burglar humped across the painting, and then the stir of a footstep as Stanhope moved out—

"From beside the mantelpiece across the room," said H.M. "There's Stanhope, in pyjamas, slippers, and heavy blue wool dressing gown. His enemy has walked bang into the trap."

H.M. pointed a stubby finger.

"Looky here. Wouldn't the evidence of the fingerprints alone have told you Stanhope wasn't the burglar?

"I stood in that dining room yesterday. I saw the place marked and blazed with smudges of gray fingerprint-powder. They led, like an Indian trail in Fenimore Cooper, in a diagonal line from the mantelpiece across to the sideboard. Stanhope's fingerprints on the center table. Stanhope's prints on the sideboard. Stanhope's prints on the handle of the fruit-knife.

"But remember: the *burglar* was wearin' gloves. If Stanhope was the burglar, how in Tartarus did his prints get all over the place? Especially since other witnesses swore that earlier in the evening, he hadn't as much as touched the sideboard, let alone mess about with the table and the mantelpiece."

"That's true enough," snarled Buller Naseby.

"So, my children. You can see what happened.

"Dwight said somethin' like 'Now, you so-and-so, I've got you. Just wait till I rouse the house.' And he went for Mr. James with both hands.

"That wasn't very sensible of him. Our Raffles was twenty years younger and a good deal stronger. He got one hard round Stanhope's mouth, and the other round his body. On the sideboard was the fruit-knife. My guess is that it'd been knocked out of the fruit-bowl when the burglar hoisted down the picture, and Stanhope could see it by the light of the torch. Stanhope grabbed it up and struck out instinctively, with his right hand, for the other chap's left breast.

"He gashed the burglar. It wasn't a deep cut. It wasn't a dangerous cut. But it bled like billy-o. Our Raffles has got the usual bully's fondness for reprisals. He wrenched Stanhope's wrist round, caught the knife as it fell, and stabbed Stanhope—as he thought—to the heart.

"Then, when the man was down . . ."

"Please, for God's sake!" cried Eleanor.

"I'm sorry, my wench. There it is."

Christabel, though she had gone white, remained steady.

"Tennis shoes," Christabel said. "Those light bruises round

the head, as though they'd been made by somebody smallish or of rather light weight. It was because the burglar wore . . ."

H.M. sniffed.

"That's right, ma'am. However enraged you are, you try kickin' with tennis shoes on, and you'll suffer a good deal more than you give. But the burglar had to have an outlet. He got better results by stampin' on a helpless man."

"Steady on, sir," Nick said quietly.

"No, son. If they hear now what a delightful person they knew, other things will hurt less later."

"Go on, Sir Henry," Christabel told him with complete calm.

"Well! Now that he's cool again, the burglar's in a pretty awful position. He can see that right enough. Murder, hey? And what's done for him is . . ."

"Blood," said Betty.

"Exactly. His own blood is all over his clothes. His original plan would have been simple: he'd have pinched the El Greco, hidden it smack in this house, and waited to remove it later. Even if the police suspect an inside job, even if they search the house, even if they find the picture, still there'd have been no evidence to show who took it.

"But this is different. This is murder. And how are you goin' to hide a complete blood-stained outfit, together with a nasty gash in your own chest?

"Wait! Hold on! Inspiration!

"There's the victim, lying apparently dead. The victim's dressing gown has come open in the fight, as dressing gowns do. The wound hasn't bled more than a drop or two. In fact, only the pyjama coat has been pierced by the knife. To most people's eyes, one dressing gown and pyjama suit looks very much like another.

"So . . .

"Cor, what an inspiration! Stanhope's hard up. His pictures must be insured. Fake burglary. If *he's* found in the incriminatin' outfit, that will both alter and save the whole situation. I don't suppose," added H.M., shaking his head, "a would-be murderer has ever got rid of blood-stained clothes so neatly or so naturally as by puttin' 'em on his victim.

"So Mr. Vincent James made the change-over. There was nothin' that could be traced to him, even the wrist-watch. In the pocket of Stanhope's dressing gown, he found one of Dwight's handkerchiefs and a couple of old letters that Dwight had shoved there after readin' them in the morning: as a good many of us do. He included these.

"But one thing bothered him—his own wound. He'd staunched a good deal of the bleedin' with his own handkerchief, but you can't keep holdin' it there. So, from the roll of surgical adhesive tape, he cut off a couple of long strips and fastened the handkerchief to his chest with 'em. Then he put on Stanhope's pyjamas and dressing gown."

"Wait!" interrupted Christabel with the same inhuman calm.

"Yes, ma'am?"

"That terrific crash of silverware in the middle of the night. I didn't hear it, but everybody else did. Wasn't that—?"

"Caused by their fight?" said H.M. "Oh, no! That was the last act, the brimmin' jugful. I was comin' to it."

(Still Vincent James did not move or speak.)

"The burglar, I estimate, got into the dining room about a quarter past three. The alarm of falling silver didn't happen until three-twenty-eight. Allowin' ample leeway for the exchange of clothes.

"Y' see, that clever gentleman tried to make the illusion just a little too good. But he had the right idea, at that. At all costs, he'd got to prevent anybody suspecting that the corpse wasn't wearing the right clothes. Once anybody did, he was dished.

"How to do that? Easy! If you hear a damn great wallop of clashing objects, and go down to find somebody laid out in a struggle, you naturally think it was caused by the struggle. So (d'ye follow?) it never occurs to you that there'd have been *time* for anybody to change clothes.

"Actually, in my opinion, the silver or the electric torch hadn't been touched by the real fight. Raffles there piled a great towerin' heap of it on the edge of the sideboard. (A lot of the pieces were nastily scratched afterwards. They wouldn't have been, just by fallin' on that thick carpet. It looked as though they'd landed smack-bang on top of each other, all in the same place.)

"Now he was ready. He put out the torch and shoved it under the victim. He gave the pile of silver a push, and was out of the window and up that rope before the noise had stopped clatterin' below.

"It wasn't a bad spur-of-the-moment alibi either."

Nick spoke bitterly.

"No," Nick agreed, "it wasn't. Before I could collect what wits I have, he had time to make the bed springs creak in his room, and turn on the light to ask me if I'd heard anything."

(For just a fraction of a second, now, he saw the edge of a contemptuous smile flash across Vince's mouth.)

153

"But do you remember later, Mrs. Stanhope?" Nick demanded. "When he came downstairs to the dining room, carrying a poker?"

Christabel sat up.

"Wait!" said Christabel. "He kept running his hand inside the left breast of his dressing gown . . ."

"Yes. Like this," said Nick. "And holding it there. When he was looking at my warrant card, I thought something must be hurting him. His wound, of course. Not an hour after that, I went to wash my face in the bathroom between our two bedrooms. And there was a reddish sediment at the bottom of the washbowl."

"Blood again?"

"No doubt about it. While I first went down to investigate the crash, he sponged his chest and dressed the wound again. But, of course, I couldn't see it at the time. He also wound up the fire-escape rope again before Larkin had a look round."

Another voice spoke.

"He was playing table tennis," said Eleanor. "Or he'd been playing table tennis. Yesterday." Her eyes looked back, in a kind of frenzy, at the past. She made illustrative gestures. "He asked if I wanted to play billiards."

"Really, Eleanor . . ."

"Please, Christabel! He picked up that heavy ping-pong table and heaved it up in the air. All of a sudden his face went so white I asked if anything was hurting him. He said only memory. Then he came over to me and—"

"Steady," interposed Betty.

Eleanor moved forward, stumbling among the folding chairs. Still another chair got in her way, and she flung it aside. Dr. Clements, looking a picture of misery, backed out of her path.

"Vince James, look at me!"

"Yes, old girl?" said Vince calmly.

"Tell me one thing. Did you kick him and beat him while he was down? Did you?"

A slight frown wrinkled Vince's forehead. He straightened up, and moved out on the stage until he was looking down at her in a slow, meditative, whimsically smiling way. There was only a slight uncertain strain round his eyes; no man, you would have said, had his nerves under better control.

"Do you honestly think, old girl, that I'd do a thing like that?"

And he smiled again.

This was the point when there appeared, at the rear of the

stage behind Vince's back, the homely but reassuring face of Commander Dawson.

The Commander, clearly, had heard not a word of all this. He had been completely absorbed in messing about with the mechanism of the trap; and he had only come up, by the stairs, when his former companion disappeared. The stage lights were in Commander Dawson's eyes. He saw little beyond Vince's back.

"Tell me!" said Eleanor. "Tell me!"

And, to add a last twist to human embarrassment, the tears were running down her face.

Christabel was staring at H.M.

"Let me understand you," Christabel said. "After the stabbing, this paragon of impudence—" she pointed to Vince —"actually walked downstairs with us wearing poor Dwight's pyjamas and blue wool dressing gown?"

"And slippers," said H.M. "Did you notice? Naturally not. Didn't I tell you people never notice quiet-colored dressing gowns?"

"But—"

"Yesterday, y'see, he sneaked the dressing gown and slippers back to Dwight's dressing room. Don't you remember? Hamley swore the dressing gown was missing that morning, but turned up before night. That was because the wardrobe cupboard was locked up until afternoon, with the burglin' clothes inside. So Raffles couldn't put back the dressing gown until he found the cupboard unlocked again.

"How do I know that? Because they gave *me* the damn dressing gown and slippers to wear last night! Burn me, when I sat by that library fire I thought about all sorts of things.

"The pyjamas, with the knife-cut in 'em and the microscopic traces of blood, were different. He kept those. He thought an extra pair of pyjamas wouldn't be noticed. But it was a silly-ass thing to do. They've been found in his dressing table. Larkin has had the laundry marks compared. They're Dwight Stanhope's."

Eleanor had not taken her eyes from Vince.

"Tell me!" she insisted.

Vince regarded her gently.

Commander Dawson, in the background, was puzzled by this emotional uproar. Unseen and unheard, he approached and put his hand lightly on Vince's shoulder.

"I say, old man—" he began.

And that did it.

There is no limit, perhaps, to what the nerves can stand when

155

their concentration is in one direction, when their whole taut energy is poured into a single piece of acting, when their effort is to hold what they see ahead. But let a breath disturb them from an unexpected direction, and there may occur what occurred then.

"Take your hand off me," a voice screamed.

Vincent James, six-feet-one and fast as a panther, turned and struck twice: left to the body and right to the face. Commander Dawson, taking it with his hands down, was flung backwards into the conjuring apparatus. He staggered, righted himself, fell forward on hand and knee, and remained swaying before he could balance.

While you might have counted ten, there was dead silence. Commander Dawson, drawing in his breath, put one hand on the silvered shaft of a table to steady himself.

H.M. looked at Eleanor.

"There's your answer, my wench," he said.

The look of dazed astonishment began to fade from the Commander's eyes. His color receded slowly, showing the ooze of a knuckle-mark between nostril and mouth.

"You damned swine," said the Commander, and straightened up. "You may be able to break me in two, but I'm going to—"

Nick was on the stage in two strides, dodging between them. He got Commander Dawson, and held him.

"No! Steady! Take it easy!"

"He'd better not," said Vince, who was as white as Christabel herself.

It was Betty who spoke: not loudly, but they all heard it.

"Eleanor, if you care so much about what Vince did, why are you wearing that ring?"

"What's the matter with the bloke?" Commander Dawson was raving. "Is he off his head? You come up to tell him something, and he turns round and lands you one." Abruptly the Commander stopped. All traces of raving were checked. His tense shoulders relaxed under Nick's grip. *"What ring?"* he said.

"You idiot," stormed Eleanor, extending her left hand. "I've been wearing your blasted ring all day, and you've never noticed it. So much for *my* romantic ideas! Do you think I c-care about him? I've been cr-crying over what an idiot I was, and what a c-cloth-headed crazy person you were, and seeing how far I could hurt myself for ever thinking s-seriously about him."

The Commander opened, shut, and opened his eyes.

"Excuse me," he said politely to Nick; and was over the edge of the stage in one bound.

156

"Gettin' on your nerves a bit, son?" H.M. said to Vince.

H.M. returned his attention to Christabel.

"About the attempted murder, there's not much more to tell. All that worried Master James afterwards, I think, is whether he ought to see a doctor about that gash of his, and how he could explain it if he did. I admit I dunno why he came to me today with some weird offer to tell me something about doctors—"

Nick intervened here.

"I can explain it, sir. He was muttering about a doctor before he went to sleep last night. I heard him, and he must have known I did. So he decided to invent some yarn, in case anybody asked why he was interested in—"

"Diamonds!" the Commander was heard to declare. "Diamonds, definitely, for the real engagement ring. Didn't I say that's what it would be?"

Nobody paid any attention except Eleanor.

"When Nick Wood," pursued H.M., "tumbled to the fact that Dwight Stanhope didn't leave the house, there was only one conclusion for me or him. There'd been an exchange of clothes inside the house; and, since the only person whose clothes would have fitted Stanhope was Vincent James . . . well, that tore it."

Nick's face was bitter.

"Do you remember—" he glanced at Betty—"when you and I were up here on Thursday night, hidden in the beignoir?"

"Don't I!" said Betty.

"Your father and Mr. Naseby came in. I took a quick look out, and said, 'It's Vince . . . no, by George, it's your father.' I could kick myself for not seeing it sooner."

"My dear," retorted Betty loyally, "I can't see you did very badly, with just forty-eight hours to work in."

H.M. held up his hand. His air was embarrassed and apologetic.

"But, d'ye see, all this had to be proved. Find out if Vincent James really has got a bandaged wound in his chest, and you can write your Q.E.D.

"But that's a bit difficult. Spyin' won't get you anywhere. And you can't very well jump on a man and start tearin' off his waistcoat and shirt to investigate; not, at least, with the feller over there." He screwed up his face in an expression almost as hideous as that of the Great Kafoozalum.

"Wait!" cried Betty.

"Yes, my wench?"

"You stood Vince up in front of all those children this

afternoon. You put your hand inside his waistcoat. To their uproarious delight, you produced yards and yards of colored ribbon. . . . Was that the game?"

"Uh-huh," said H.M. simply. "No fight. No fuss. No suspicion." He peered round at Vince. "Or was there, son? You'll have to take your shirt off at the police station."

Christabel was thinking.

"I'll admit," she told them in a cold, steady voice, "I've sometimes wondered whether Mr. James could be as dense as he seemed. Just when you had decided he was stupid, he said something so shrewd that you wondered if he'd said it by accident. I was wondering last night, before I went to bed, whether he mightn't be a very clever man. You see, I knew he'd originally been a medical student . . ."

Eleanor swung round from Commander Dawson.

"Oh, to the devil with it!" Eleanor said. "I don't think he's so clever. He said himself that all he remembered about medicine was the funny bits. Like the saucer."

Buller Naseby got slowly to his feet.

"What saucer?" rasped Mr. Naseby, with difficulty in his throat.

"Steady!" roared H.M.

Eleanor was puzzled. "Just a test he once told me about. Only doctors and policemen know it, as a rule. It's to make sure somebody is really dead."

"To make sure . . ." Mr. Naseby began.

"Isn't that right, Dr. Clements?" asked Eleanor.

The physician moistened his lips.

"The test," Dr. Clements acknowledged, "is not well-known like the test of holding a mirror or a plain glass to the lips to find the smallest trace of breathing. But it is just as effective, perhaps, more so. If no mirror or smooth glass is at hand . . ."

Mr. Naseby's eyes opened.

"No mirror," he said. "Cut-glass pitcher. Bakelite drinking cup."

"Take an ordinary saucer," said Dr. Clements, "fill it to the brim with water, and place it on the chest of the person in doubtful condition. If there is the slightest tremor in the water, traces of life remain. If not—"

"I see," observed Mr. Naseby in a piercing voice. "He had to be *very* sure the second time."

What most of them made of this cryptic observation Nick could not tell. But it was no pleasant one. He saw Christabel turn her head; he saw her clasped hands tighten so that white marks showed above the pink-blooded nails.

"And," said Mr. Naseby, "he was frightened away by Larkin before he could remove the saucer."

Dr. Clements popped up from his chair.

"The end," he announced, "was completely without pain. You might say, dear lady, that he died in his sleep."

Vincent James took another step backwards.

No word of explanation was spoken. None was needed. The faces of three women were slowly turned round towards one tall figure and one ugly, frightened pair of eyes.

H.M. drew a slow, wheezy breath. His cigar had gone out again, and he dropped it on the carpet. But it was the faces of three women which Vincent could not stand.

"You're not going to arrest me," he said. "Nobody's going to arrest *me*."

"Look out!" shouted Commander Dawson.

Vince's movements were again so blindingly quick that Nick had no more than lunged forward when the door to the sundeck boomed and banged shut again.

"Let him go, son," said H.M. wearily. "He can't get away. I locked the door to the floor below when we came up. Here's the key. He can't get away."

"Can't he get away," snarled Mr. Naseby, "if he tries it by way of the roof?"

"No. You remember—"

"The roof," said Betty.

Nick stared back at her; and it was perhaps ten seconds before he remembered a certain scene that afternoon, of an icy wind and an open door. Then he plunged out towards the sundeck.

The last light in the sky had gone. Dim electric bulbs in the roof of the passage were reflected in black glass. The white paint had a funereal dullness. And, a little way along where the passage curved, there was another open door faintly creaking in another icy wind.

Outside, the lights showed two, three, four footprints clearly printed in the snow, before the ugly trampling of a frenzied man was printed there too, as he plodded and churned and screamed when the whole mass of snow began to slide. But no cry came. No call for help was heard. Nothing more.

Nick turned round and walked very slowly back to the theater.

All those in the room of memory were on their feet. Commander Dawson's arms were round Eleanor, whose head was on his breast, and she held him tightly. Betty moved to Nick's side. Christabel alone was leaving them. As she passed them, Sir Henry Merrivale touched her gently on the arm.

"Your daughter and your step-daughter," he said, "are goin' to be very happy. Don't you think, ma'am, that one day you can be happy too?"

And he stood aside, saying no more, while Christabel Stanhope went downstairs to find a new life.

THE END